GRIT and SILVER

Joanna Heywood

Typeset in Baskerville

Editing, design, typesetting and publishing by UK Book Publishing

www.ukbookpublishing.com

ISBN: 978-1-913179-84-7

Cover illustrations: Coca plant by Becky Brown

GRIT and SILVER

Introduction

Driven by a particularly savage interpretation of China's Maoist revolution, the Communist Party of Peru, also known as Shining Path, launched a civil war in the 1980s and 1990s led by a university professor, Abimael Guzmán and his wife, Augusta la Torre. The conflict terrorized Peru with assassinations, bombings, beheadings, and massacres, costing 70,000 lives and leaving many more damaged by emotional and physical scars. Entangled in this conflict, many of Peru's farmers were forced to grow a large proportion of the world's cocaine, trapped in a circle of poverty and dependence on drug traffickers.

The origins of this story go back to the early 2000s, when the author travelled to Peru fresh from university. She volunteered for a year in Lima under the supervision of a missionary who introduced her to life in the slums. There, she met communities of people facing the odds together. She also met most of the women featured in this book.

Inspired to stay on, she lived in Peru for four years during which she set up a social enterprise to help women access meaningful employment. She was struck by the lack of choices women faced – generally motherhood and exploitation kept them trapped in poverty. Yet all these women were striving for something better for their families, and they possessed an unquenchable energy and drive to go forwards. All the women had stories of tragedy, violence, and hope. All had grown up in rural areas steeped in poverty, local myths, and ancestral traditions – and all had escaped to the city in search of a better life.

Those impressions never left her, but they seemed too big to put into writing, and it took fifteen years before she overcame the fear of capturing these women's stories in a book.

This book is based on true stories and most names and places have been changed.

Part I – Maria's Story

Pusanga

(Love Potion)

-I-

I used to love walking home from school in the small town of
Tingo Maria to our farmstead, deep in the Amazon jungle.
As I trudged along the dirt track after a day at school leaving
the bustling town behind me, the trees would get denser and
start closing in, gradually blanking out the sounds and smells
of traffic and motorbikes and the busy market. Instead, I
would immerse myself in the hum of frogs and bush crickets,
as the light turned from bright harsh white to soft green and
the intoxicating smells of the undergrowth filled my nostrils
– rich, damp earth and a thousand plants and barks.

Most of my school friends lived in Tingo Maria itself and
feared going into the undergrowth alone. But I loved it. "One
day you will get caught by the Sachamama and she will eat
you alive," they warned me. This huge, solitary boa lives in
the deepest jungle marshes, and at certain points of her life,
every hundred years or so, she needs to put on weight and sets
out looking for meat. The swishing of her huge tail makes the
same sound as the Huallaga river, so she easily catches out

the poor, ignorant animals and people who cross her path. After giving her prey a deadly squeeze, she stretches open her jaws, engulfs it whole by crushing its bones, and slithers back into the scrub to enjoy a century-long digestive nap. Jungle dwellers live in fear of her, and whisper about her to their children at bedtime. But I never came across the Sachamama, and if I did, she wasn't hungry.

It would take me about an hour to hug the curves of the Huallaga river under the lush canopy of the rainforest to reach our family's plot of land. It stood on a small clearing surrounded with tall açai palm trees, their clusters of berries drooping like shocks of black hair. As I got closer to our dilapidated wooden house in the middle of the clearing, a flicker of fear would lick the pit of my stomach. Would my father be sober? Would he be calm, sitting on the porch sharpening his machete against a rough tree stub? Or as so often, would I find him indoors, crimson-faced and yelling about some tiny thing my mother had done wrong? Or worse, lashing out as she cowered in a corner of the room shielding herself against his blows with a threadbare dish cloth?

"You useless woman, you can't even cook a meal properly!" he would rant, picking at a minor fault in his meal.

"My mother is a very good cook." I would glare at him from the other side of the room with clenched fists. But he hated it when I defended her – "And what would you know, you can't even fry an egg! You're always outdoors like a wild animal.

5

At least make yourself useful and go and fetch some water from the river."

As I wandered down with the jerry cans, I would reflect on the word Pusanga. A word you often hear mentioned in our community. It means the perfume of love. My mother said that was what my father had used to make her fall in love with him many years earlier – a shamanic spell which drew her irresistibly to him. She was very young – barely fifteen, when he had set eyes on her bathing in the Huallaga river during a raging storm, and he had instantly decided that she was the one.

She was light-skinned and plump and looked slightly angelic, with her shy almond-shaped eyes and pearly white teeth. He approached her, smiling broadly and confidently, but she showed him no interest. Anyway, she was promised to someone else – a distant cousin in a nearby village. Unfazed, my father went to see the local witch, Dona Elvira, who concocted a potion from dried and powdered plants such as arrowroot, dry love and toucan's tongue, mixed with others whose names she would not reveal to the uninitiated.

My mother never actually told me how she came to drink the pusanga, but its effect was undeniable – around midnight that same night she became restless and was overcome with a fever. She told her parents that her head would explode unless she could run out into the night and straight into my father's arms. Her family soon realised that she had been bewitched and tied her to the bed for a couple of days in the hope that the spell would pass. "Rub her skin with raw onion," suggested a neighbour, "or rub a guinea pig over her body, it will absorb the evil and die". But after a few hours my mother broke free and, leaping from her bed, she rushed to find my father.

Very soon the effect of the pusanga began to wear off. My father asked my mother to show him the "proof of her love" but in her youthful innocence she did not know what he meant. He tore her clothes off, and she fought back in distress, but in the end, he got what he wanted. My mother never trusted him after that, but she accepted her fate, as so many women did. My mother's father was furious about the pusanga and blamed my mother for letting it happen. But in the end, he allowed the romance because, as he said to my mother, "You can't just go from man to man." Reluctant blessings were granted and my father and his soon-to-be son in law shook hands. But my father was never really accepted by my mother's family – he did not own any land and rented a small plot from his uncle, scarcely making a living.

Despite my father's shortcomings, he never laid hands on me and I grew up quite happily, spending as much time out of the house as I could when I wasn't at school, and fending for myself. I soon learnt to ride a horse through the jungle, bare backed and fearless. I would gallop off into the undergrowth for hours on my own, stray branches scratching my back, enjoying how the vegetation twisted and writhed all around me as my horse squelched through the humming bog. I would return home before nightfall as the bats started to dart amongst the thick trees. I would bring strange and wonderful fruits home which I had swiped off the trees with my coarse machete.

"Be careful walking through the forest," my father would say. "There are dangerous men out there, more dangerous than the Sachamama boa." But he never told me who these dangerous men were and why they would go after me. The only clear thing we had been taught was to fear the North Americans – tall, blond people called *gringos*. At school we were taught that they were cannibals who would make a necklace from your teeth and bones.

When I got back from my trips to the forest, my mother would always be waiting up for me with a plate of dinner, anxious about the anacondas and poisonous dart frogs which came out at night. She would sit with me while I ate, listening to my stories and tasting some of the fruits I had brought home. Our favourite was the juicy guava, full of tiny worms which were barely visible unless we put them right next to the oil lamp. We also loved the long, bean-like pacaya which revealed its sweet fluffy fruit like baby clouds, and the bumpy noni which we sprinkled with salt. I dreamed of eating creamy avocado, but this was out of bounds. "Girls can't eat avocado until they are married, as it reveals what it's like to be with a man," my mother would explain.

Three months after my parents were married, my father

had started beating my mother for failing to get pregnant. Eventually she had her first baby, but it died after just twelve hours. As you gave birth the community would sit outside the house drinking coffee and waiting for the news. If the baby were born healthy, the neighbours would get ready to kill their best chickens to celebrate the joyous arrival.

But if the baby died, they would say "Lazy girl, she must have bad blood". For my poor mother it was no different. Nobody spoke to her for days after her baby died, and she quietly buried her stillborn child and her grief, alone under a cedar tree.

Three years and several miscarriages later I was finally born, their first child, after my mother had endured eight days of labour pains. The chickens were slaughtered and eaten with great gusto, washed down with lashings of firewater, and a raucous crowd descended to the river to dispose of the placenta and summon good luck for all our futures.

Though my mother had never been to school she was skilled and wise, and loved imparting her knowledge to me. When my father was out, we would sit together happily, and after she had finished plucking the chickens or pounding the cassava, she would tell me all about the jungle and its secrets.

My mother knew how to use cedar bark to cure a fever, and its resin as a sweet-smelling insect repellent.

"Rub your hand over the tree and the bugs won't bite you" she would show me.

She told me how a concoction of mashed banana had saved Uncle Eduardo from losing his foot from a crocodile bite. She knew which leaves to pick if you wanted your periods to stop for six months, and which ones to spread on a snake bite for instant relief. If she had time on her hands, which was rare, she would join me on my forest walks and help me recognise the cocona fruit and hunt down charapita chillies or wild coriander. She pointed out which stalks to crush to relieve dry, itchy eyes, and which trees' hollowed out branches hid reserves of pure, drinkable water.

"Mama, how do you know all these things?" I would ask repeatedly.

"These are the jungle's remedies," she replied, a spark of mischief lighting her shy eyes. "The forest is sacred and imbued with spirits, and you have to listen to them if you want to understand them."

Apart from the curative virtues of plants, my mother taught me to love animals, and spoiled me with new pets whenever she had a chance. First came a dog called Alan Garcia, named after our president of the time. Alan had dozens of fleas, which I proceeded to name individually.

"Bathe him in fish milk to kill the fleas," my mother suggested helpfully.

But the fish milk turned out to be toxic and poor Alan died after his bath. I buried him under a small cross and a wreath of açai branches. Soon after Alan died, I was consoled by a jungle rabbit, dark brown and tiny with black stripes and normally eaten in stew. My mother also produced a cat named Pancho and a tamed blue macaw, who would feast on sweet mango and slept next to me making gentle grunting noises. One night, lulled into a particularly deep slumber, I rolled over and squashed the poor bird in my sleep. Keen to help me get over my many losses, my mother soon caught me my very own pichico pygmy monkey, smaller than my hand, who sent me to sleep at night by nit-picking through my hair.

Catching monkeys was easy – they loved salt and would not bite when you held your hand out for them to lick it. After that, they would just follow you around. They knew when a woman was pregnant and held their tiny arms to their tummies, puffing them out then tapping the unfortunate woman's stomach for the whole world to see. It was difficult to hide your pregnancy from people if there was a chattering pet monkey around. I made my pichico monkey small clothes and he would brush his teeth with his own child size toothbrush. He behaved like a person, screeching to demand food, and asking for toilet paper after doing his business. He became a close friend and comforted me if I cried after my parents' rows.

One day I came home to find my pichico monkey hanging from one of the beams of our hut, limp and forlorn with his tiny tongue hanging out and a swollen belly. I never knew if he had killed himself or if someone had got rid of him.

I cried inconsolably every time one of my pets died. But my father was oblivious to my grief.

"What do you need all these animals for?" he would grumble impatiently. "Animals are for eating." But I loved these creatures and the dense jungle they came from, with all my heart.

My parents had three more children before my eighth birthday – my younger brothers Jorge, Milder and Roosevelt. They tumbled into the world and wandered around dirty and barefooted until their baptisms. Then, as tradition dictated, my mother wearily found them godparents to buy them shoes and teach them to be good Catholics.

My brothers' godparents were hastily found – whoever was Catholic and could afford to buy shoes would do the trick. But I got lucky with my godmother. Mercedes was a teacher at my school. She had two sons of her own but no daughter, and she treated me like one of her own children. She bought me shoes but also new clothes, schoolbooks, and a brand-new satchel, shipped all the way from Lima. Mercedes knew that my parents were poor, and how my father treated my mother.

When I was eight, I told Mercedes how much my father drank and how angry it made him, and she invited me to live with her family in Tingo Maria for a while. I stayed at her house for eight years. There was a TV set in her living room, which blasted out endless episodes of tortured Venezuelan soap operas. Our farmstead had no electricity, let alone a TV, and the attraction proved difficult to resist. Mercedes taught me to read and write properly, which few girls around me could do. Mercedes told me to stand up for myself, and that women were not the property of men.

"Men often carry guns and use violence," she would teach me, "but if you learn to use your intelligence, and learn to read and write, you will be more intelligent than any man and you will always win."

My mother missed me and was sad that I had left but I visited often, bringing her fruit and exciting gossip from town, and reading to her from a book so that she could be proud of my achievements.

Tingo Maria was a sleepy town for many years, and TV and Venezuelan soaps our only insight into the world beyond. But the drug traffickers (whom we called the narcos) and the communists brought an end to that. For as long as I could remember people had been talking about the growing conflict, and nearly everyone had lost a relative or been affected somehow. But there was not just one conflict – there were many and they were all tangled up and you never really knew which one people were talking about. The narcos fought the narcos, the narcos fought the army, the army fought the communist terrorists and the communist terrorists denied anything they did was terrorism, whilst also fighting amongst themselves.

People talked a lot about fear and danger in those days, but I was not afraid. I had seen my mother cowering from my father, and I had sworn to myself that one day I would be strong enough to defend her and to get my own back for the way she had been treated.

-2-

When I turned fifteen, my mother encouraged me to eat scaly aguaje fruit, which was known as the curvy fruit and supposedly helped women gain an hourglass figure. But I refused, instead taking up smoking and swearing, wearing a cap, and dressing like a man. Girls of my age were already starting to have children, and many had been taken out of school aged thirteen and told they were old enough to have husbands.

Not that staying at school necessarily helped. Apart from teaching us to read and write, it mainly served to fill our heads with legends and nonsense. We were taught that babies were delivered by plane, and not to question this. A fresh-faced new teacher came to the village and started trying to teach us how babies were really born. She was fired without delay. Mercedes tried to stand up for her, but the head teacher was adamant – school was not the place to be encouraging depravity.

My father resented me for living the high life with Mercedes' family, and for talking about gaining an education. He called me pretentious and when I came home to visit my mother he would sneer at me at the dinner table.

"Here we eat with a spoon, not with a knife and fork like those people," he mocked.

But the arrangement suited him financially and gave him one less mouth to feed. And besides, despite his reluctance he must have had some good intentions and hopes for me. "I don't want you growing up a brute like us," he would remind me as I headed back off towards Tingo Maria after each visit.

I would probably have stayed at Mercedes' house for many more years given the chance, as it suited me well to be away from my father – and I was getting hooked on Venezuelan soaps. But one day tragedy struck and forced me back home to support my mother.

My brother Jorge, by then a sweet twelve-year-old with yellow eyes, who always offered people help carrying their water from the river, was taken ill with the jungle fever. After eleven days my mother realised that spreading cedar bark on his skin wasn't working, and that the poor boy was burning up.

She took him into town but could not afford the cost of a hospital stay and was turned away by an apologetic nurse. Alongside the hospital was the pungent smelling street where witch doctors could be found, amongst stalls and tiny shops selling herbs and unguents. The healers' street offered cheaper alternatives to hospital treatment and was conveniently located to receive desperate patients and their families.

The healer woman took one look at my brother and prescribed fresh bull blood. "The strength of the bull will fight the fever and cure him," she explained to my panic-stricken mother, producing a small plastic pouch full of dark red liquid. Jorge drank the contents of the pouch and died a few hours later in my mother's arms. I bid farewell to Mercedes and her family and moved back in with my parents soon after that. They had both grown grey and thin from the grief.

So there I was, back at my parents' at fifteen. While my school friends had settled into domestic life and were having babies, I swallowed my grief, pushed on my cap, and began frequenting the tiny gambling bars in the centre of town. I would return home smelling of drink and smoke – much to my mother's dismay.

I was still old enough to go to school but had lost interest in the teachers' old wives tales, preferring to drink and swear in the gambling bars, and occasionally kicking a football around with some hapless lads in town.

Tingo Maria was a standard jungle town, with a Catholic Church and municipal building set on a central square, or Arms' Square as it is unpleasantly called all over South America. A sleepy crisscross of roads fed off the square, lined with small houses improvising as corner shops – usually just a window into someone's living room with soap, cigarettes and mangos on display. The gambling shops were tucked down side streets, unlicensed and unannounced except by a few red plastic tables and chairs and the occasional crack addict slouching by the door, drifting in his parallel world.

Nobody really seemed to know where the addicts got their crack from. Drug activities were frowned upon and seen as a sign of weak character. Young boys were encouraged to gain a good education and to go far in life. Success stories were venerated, like that of Don Ruli, our local businessman who owned the town's hotel, half the market stalls, several gambling shops, and the much-frequented karaoke bar.

Don Ruli was always to be spotted practising karaoke on a Wednesday night, and had a personal orchestra that played for him most other evenings.

"When you grow up you will be rich and successful like Don Ruli," adoring mothers would whisper to their toddlers, never questioning the source of Don Ruli's fortune.

The gambling shops were rarely frequented by women, but I was good at it and would often win, spending my winnings on food which I brought home to my mother. But she would push my gifts away, dreading what would become of me in these godforsaken places.

"Why do you behave like a man?" she despaired. "Can't you get yourself a nice boy and settle down?"

I would shrug and scoff back: "What, and live like you do, locked at home and scared all of the time?"

I was adamant that I would never fall in love and suffer the same fate as my mother and contemplated becoming a nun to be on the safe side. On my way home from the gambling bars I would stop off at the Catholic church, sitting at one of the back pews with my cap in my hand. I gazed longingly at the statue of the Virgin Mary that adorned the altar, fussily decorated with lace, beads and flowers.

But the Virgin had little to say to me, or if she did wish to convey some divine truths to me, she struggled to get the words out. She remained silent and stared into space from her wooden perch. Disappointed, I instead sought the path ahead by visiting the witch, Dona Elvira. After I had paid her a few coins, she read my palm and declared I would fall in love with a tall pale outsider and travel far away. I was horrified by this news and continued my mental preparations for entering the Catholic orders.

I hated it when people told me I was beautiful. I would snap back at them – "Go away, what do you want?" – push my cap down over my hair and ride off into my beloved jungle. In the rainy season this would involve wading through the deep red mud that rose to my horse's knees, sticky and opulent – and progress was slow and slippery. But in the dry season I would go as far into the forest as I fancied, or until my horse grew tired, hypnotised by the rattling hum of cicadas, and intoxicated by heavy, humid air and green smells around us.

I did not enter the divine orders in the end. Soon before I turned eighteen, Tingo Maria was turned upside down by a shooting spree outside the Catholic church. I was near the scene at the time and heard the pop of rifle shots and panicked screams as people ducked and scrambled from the scene. Two people died in the shooting and their souls could be seen floating angrily over the square for weeks after the incident.

The army was called in, but we were hardly surprised – the nearby town of Juanjui was a hotspot for the Maoist guerrillas of the Shining Path, and it had only been a matter of time before the unrest reached our town. Scrawled messages had recently begun to appear on the walls, painted in bad spelling at the dead of night. One read: "Soldier, kill your captain and join the popular war." The narcos, the army and the communists were all at each other's throats, and we were all caught in the middle. It was difficult to say which group we hated the most – all seemed intent on killing, selling drugs, and gaining control of the country.

Around this time, the army was trying to track down a communist commander called The Leopard, who was second only in command to the leaders of the Shining Path, Comrade Guzmán and his wife Norah. The Leopard was behind the shooting spree in our town and was using the area as training ground for his guerrilla. Or at least so they said. It was always difficult to know if people were speaking the truth or making up tales to get you on their side and keep someone off their back.

To corner the Leopard and his men, a steady stream of soldiers descended on Tingo Maria, where there had hardly been any military presence before. They were everywhere, standing on our street corners, drinking in our bars, and loitering outside our schools to chat up the teenage girls. We were warned not to go out with them and there were stories that if the terrorists found any of us in cahoots with soldiers, they would kill us and leave us with our heads in the river and a sign round our necks saying: "Dogs deserve to die".

At the beginning the presence of the military disturbed us, but we soon got used to seeing them, propped on their gleaming guns and flashing their silver smiles as they attempted to seduce our women. One of them said to me: "There is a bullet in my gun and I'll kill myself if you don't kiss me..." He had striking green eyes but his acne put me off, and anyway he was a liar – I heard he said the same thing to numerous other women around town, and he never did get round to shooting himself – even though many of us turned down his advances.

These military men seemed repulsive to me, from the way they looked to the way they ate. They drank and sneered and gleamed with sweat, and their uniforms reeked of dirt and violence.

When I turned eighteen Mercedes decided I was old enough to attend a new year party in town, but that she and a friend should chaperone me to keep me out of trouble. January was the hottest month of our year, and Mercedes and her friend bobbed around to ear-splitting cumbia music and downed ice-cold beers. A tall, pale, lanky soldier invited me to dance and pulled me close. I tingled with new feelings. We danced until 4am and he walked us all home – Mercedes and her friend rather wobbly on their feet by this point. He quietly asked to see me again. His name was Gabriel, and he seemed different from the other soldiers.

The next day Mercedes nursed her hangover, mixing lemon with the foul-smelling chupusaca plant and spreading it over her face and arms. She swore it brought full and immediate recovery, and in winter she also used it to cure her rheumatism. Having regained her composure, she grabbed my arm sharply:

"Maria, I am warning you about going out with soldiers, you could end up in a ditch somewhere."

"Yes, auntie," I replied politely, my mind singing with the thought of the tall pale outsider.

I didn't see Gabriel again for a long time. His base was outside Tingo Maria and he was rarely in town. He was shy and spoke in monosyllables, but his quiet attention made me feel full of life. He was respectful towards me, holding the door open like a gentleman, asking if he could kiss me and not pushing me for more. I awaited our infrequent encounters with impatience and butterflies in my stomach.

I found out very little about Gabriel's background as he was very reserved. I bombarded him with questions about his family, but he revealed just a few short stories at once, opening gradually like a shy jacaranda flower.

The household was headed up by their mother, and Gabriel was the second child of nine, all brothers. Gabriel's father had been an evangelical pastor to start with, but got pulled into mysterious activities that made money, after eating a plant which he said the Colombians had brought over to Peru. Eating the plant had changed his character and had turned him bad.

Gabriel's family had moved to Tingo Maria to escape the communists. While a teenager, Gabriel witnessed his father's death, shot in broad daylight for becoming wealthy from these unnamed activities, and for being an imperialist dog.

At the age of eighteen, Gabriel had an identity card and his papers were in order, which was a rare thing in the jungle at that time. He enrolled in the army as fast as he possibly could, planning to get his revenge on the communists for killing his father. His mother supported the idea – the army paid well, and stable jobs were rare in this part of the world. Besides, she had eight other mouths to feed and the price of rice was out of control.

Gabriel rarely talked about what he had to do in the army, but I knew it involved shooting communists. He told me he was scared as he had to patrol the hills where The Leopard and his men hid out. This was the dreaded Red Zone where coca plants were grown and sold to be made into cocaine – which was how the communists got the money to buy their weapons.

"They protect the growers by shooting thieves who try to steal the coca leaves." Gabriel explained. "And in return, the growers pay them a tax which makes them rich. The more drugs are made, the richer the communists get and the more guns they can buy."

"But where do they buy their guns from?" I enquired.

"There is always a way to buy guns if you have money," Gabriel replied mysteriously. "Before, they used to kill policemen and soldiers to strip them of their guns, and they stole dynamite from the silver mines, but that method was too slow. Now, through the cocaine trade they have access to proper money. Do you know that half the drugs that reach the USA come from this valley?"

For a year nobody knew of my relationship with Gabriel – Mercedes appeared to have forgotten all about the whole incident at the new year dance. When I finally found the courage to tell my parents about him, I was told to "wash" as the military were deeply mistrusted. Though my father was hoping to find me a suitable match in the community, he had no friends and the people he knew owned no land, so he struggled to offer up alternative suitors.

"It could be worse, at least he isn't a narco or a terrorist," he eventually reasoned.

My mother invited Gabriel to our farmstead for lunch and seemed instantly taken with his gentle nature. They sat chewing their food in silence, kindred spirits with a mutual appreciation for silence, and for the wild girl who had brought them together.

Gabriel was more nervous about introducing me to his own mother, an intimidating lady of 42 years, who stood for no nonsense since her husband's untimely death. One morning I came across her walking towards me just outside town. I recognised her from a photograph Gabriel carried in his uniform pocket. Too intimidated to be able to face her, I swiftly climbed up to the middle branches of a nearby avocado tree. I was nimble and my escape went unnoticed, but a dog soon came to stand under the tree, barking ferociously at me. I didn't climb down until noon when the dog's owner returned, thinking I was up the tree to steal his avocados.

I told Gabriel about this incident and he laughed quietly until the tears rolled down his face. It was only a few days afterwards that he pulled out a silver ring and quietly declared his love for me.

"But you're a soldier, Gabriel," I despaired. "How can we be together?"

"I won't be a soldier for ever," he replied, a twinkle in his eye. "I will find a way to get rich and get out of the army soon."

-3-

I had fallen in love with Gabriel's quiet, mysterious nature, and as it turned out that is what I got for the rest of my days. After a few months, and much to my mother's dismay at my morals, we settled into a small room together in town. We didn't see each other much more than before – Gabriel was away patrolling the hills for days on end with his squadron. Sometimes weeks would go by without him sending news. Often people in the shops and bars in town would give vivid accounts of air and land raids they had witnessed as they went about their business or ploughed their land. They spoke of the incessant rattle of machine guns that echoed across the plains.

Increasing people were fleeing the area to seek safety in the cities. We would see them passing through on the buses, with nothing but the clothes on their backs and a few hurriedly gathered possessions. Wearily they would stop off at Don Ruli's supermarket for food and water before boarding the bus for the four-day drive to Lima. Once I chatted to a very young couple who told me their families and their whole village had been massacred, further north where the communists had firmly established their bloody grip. They were still in shock, their eyes wide as they told me of their narrow escape.

If I didn't see Gabriel for several days, I would begin to prepare myself for the imminent news of his death. But eventually he always returned, unharmed but on edge and haggard-looking, unwashed and filthy with a beard and long bedraggled hair.

"Where were you, my love?" I would cry. "I thought you were dead."

"I'll just get a haircut and a shave and then I'll tell you all about it," he would reply calmly.

Part of me craved Gabriel's company and resented these long absences, but for the most part I was content with my freedom. Loneliness, and worrying whether he was dead, were lesser evils compared with the oppression I had seen my father inflict on my mother. All my school friends had already settled into domestic life and carried numerous runny-nosed children at their hip. They spent their days cooking, cleaning pots and pounding laundry on stones in the river, bow-backed and exhausted-looking, and had aged twenty years in less than three.

I had no children yet and was as free as a hummingbird.

Besides, I had begun eating avocados, and the secrets of pleasure had finally been revealed to me – when Gabriel returned from his long travels, he would sweep me into his arms and into nights of tingling bliss.

One day Gabriel mumbled a few words about having left the army and found another job, but as usual no further information was forthcoming. On the surface our lives remained the same. Gabriel continued to disappear for days, often returning at night, and creeping into bed while I slept. I did not ask questions – it had never been in Gabriel's nature to go into the detail of his work. I contented myself with the bundles of banknotes he had started leaving on the table, tied with a sprig of bright red ladybird seeds for good luck. I assumed this influx of money must mean Gabriel had secured a serious job, and I put my own mind to rest with expediency.

I had always told Gabriel that I was not interested in money, that it was as poisonous as toucan's tongue and turned people bad. But he smiled quietly. "You won't say that when I take you shopping for new shoes with high heels." We both laughed, as he knew I was a tomboy and would wear nothing of the sort. But I did let him buy me large platefuls of fried chicken and plantain banana at the local diner. Extravagant gifts began to appear, such as a huge double bed with a swan-shaped headboard, pure white and regal. Never in my life had I seen or owned such luxury, and I took to bed for several days to enjoy my palatial furnishings.

This way of life continued for quite a while, and I felt happy, although I suspected I should probably enquire where these bundles of dollar bills were coming from. Gabriel did mention frequent trips to our local airport, which led me to contemplate two conceivable options as to the source of his growing wealth: either he had a job at the airport, and was successful in securing very generous tips, or he was being paid to ship goods to other parts of the world. There were very few import-export businesses in our area, and to the outside world our valley was known for only one thing: the planes carried coca base to the cocaine labs in Colombia. There, it was processed and shipped on to the drug-craving partygoers in North America.

I refused to confront this eventuality for a while, preferring a state of blissful denial to the idea that Gabriel might be a criminal. But one day he disappeared again, returning weeks later covered in blood and saying he had helped a friend carry a dead pig. Panicking, I began to overturn everything in our small apartment, and discovered a gun under our mattress. I stared at it, lying cold and deadly at the bottom of our pleasure nest, and I felt my small world fall apart.

I confronted Gabriel and burst into tears, insisting to know the truth, and threatening to leave that night if he continued to treat me like an idiot. He admitted calmly that he was a "narcotraficante", a drug producer. Since leaving the army he had been involved with a gang making coca base from leaves harvested in the jungle.

"I did it for us," Gabriel explained unconvincingly. "It's the only way to make some money around here, and I wanted to look after you."

"But I don't need looking after, and I don't want any money. Can't you see you're going to get us killed? And then what will we do with all that cash?"

Gabriel explained that there was no way out – once you were in, the gang looked out for you and expected unwavering loyalty. "I know where everything is, how the stuff is made. I know who all the people are. I just can't get out of this now. You have to believe me, Maria."

I believed him, and we swore our undying love to each other. I also swore complete silence, understanding that a failure to protect Gabriel's secrets would likely result in us getting killed soon afterwards.

Now I knew the awful truth. If I did not seem to support Gabriel, his gang could accuse me of betrayal. The most useful thing I could do was to get involved and help out, so a few days later we sped into the jungle on Gabriel's motorbike, where I was initiated into the intricacies of production.

We slid along the mud paths, with a few jerry cans strapped to the back of the bike which Gabriel filled at the petrol station. Deep into the undergrowth we reached a small clearing, a shabby tarpaulin and some wooden planks the only visible equipment. A group of men and women from nearby farms had gathered with five or six large sacks of coca leaves, freshly picked from their farmsteads.

We spread the leaves out to dry for half a day, thousands of harmless-looking green halfmoons. Then we chopped them into small pieces with a string trimmer, sprinkling them with powdered cement and soaking them in several gallons of petrol overnight. "To release the alkaloid," they explained.

We camped out to watch over the process, chatting and drinking beer while two or three of the men kept guard and looked out for rival gangs or the army. By the morning I was drunk and rather enjoying myself, but Gabriel decided to take me home. "The process gets smelly and dangerous now," he explained.

When the petrol was removed, Gabriel explained as we sped on our way, the leaves would be pressed for remaining liquid and discarded. Then a bucket of battery acid would be poured on, resulting in a tarpaulin sized amount of murky-looking smelly liquid. A sprinkle of powdered caustic soda and the gloop would be duly filtered through a cloth. The resulting material, when dried into a crumbly yellow block, was called pasta or base. It was sold on to the Colombians, leaving the remains of the petrol and acid to seep into Mother Earth. Months later, I was told, a rich American would buy the final product on a street corner in New York for thirty times the production price.

Neither the farmers growing the leaves, nor Gabriel and his accomplices, could understand what all the fuss was about, and why the Americans were so desperate to buy this stuff. None of them had ever tried smoking it and they did not ever intend to. They were terrified of it, having seen the awful ingredients that went into the mix. In fact, we felt rather sorry for these young Americans who were addicted to such a foul brew.

But the army did seem to care, and its helicopters hummed and swept over the hills like angry cicadas, spreading liquid weed killer in their wake to wipe out the coca plants. The farmers told us how they suffered from these toxic fumes. They said they had seen rivers and lakes turned red with chemicals, and that their crops and animals were all dying.

Once the crumbly yellow blocks were ready, Gabriel would take the goods to the airport, taking many risks along the way. At any moment he knew he might get gunned down by the army or by rival drug gangs, but also by the tall Americans – the most terrifying enemies of all. Since childhood we had been told about these fearsome giants and of how they would attack you and leave your hands or feet behind in the bush. They would take the rest of your body away to drain it of its fat, which they sold on to the planes as airline fuel. I had never heard of anyone in our community enduring such a ghastly fate, but the stories continued to be told so we assumed them to be true. "Behave, or the Americans will get you," my school friends would say to their runny-nosed toddlers, who ran off screaming in terror.

After a few months, a rival Colombian gang realised that Gabriel used to be in the army and came round to threaten him with death unless he gave them vast sums of money. Gabriel informed me of this in his usual composed manner one night, then left me alone in our lodgings – telling me to stay there and to be very quiet. By midnight all the lights were out – there was a curfew imposed by the President since the beginning of the unrest, so that the army could get on with the business of dropping bombs without seeing a thing.

I lay on our bed terrified as I waited for Gabriel's return, hoping for the pounding in my chest to die down. We had no blinds or curtains on the window, and I awoke to a man standing outside the window, shining a torch, and yelling to be let in. I ducked under cover thinking that he would kill me, praying for mercy and crying for God's forgiveness for every sin I had ever committed. I thought the man would break the window and waited, powerless and trembling under our voluminous swan bed. At five in the morning Gabriel returned but the man had left. Having noted my distress, Gabriel lay down for a few hours' rest. He promised me that we would be safe and that all would be well, but the following night the same thing happened, and I demanded an explanation.

"Many of the competing producer gangs are now dead or in prison," Gabriel explained. "I suppose they are after us next."

The situation had become untenable and we left our few belongings, including the ludicrous bed, just as they stood, and took to the hills on Gabriel's motorbike. For a few days we hid in the jungle, sinking into mud up to our ankles, diving into the bushes and lying panting every time a car would pass for fear of being found and shot.

As we huddled together in the humming undergrowth, we discussed our options and concluded that a proper escape was the only way forward.

"I have family in Lima," Gabriel offered. "We can start again there."

We paid a final visit to my village, staying for five days in the undergrowth nearby and visiting my parents at mealtimes. My mother was delighted to see me and smothered me with kisses and platefuls of fried chicken, but my father was sombre. He mistrusted our vague reasons for being there, and for staying away at nightfall.

"Some kind of trouble you must have got yourself into," he grumbled. "I knew you would come to no good with that soldier."

Spending my last moments with my mother reminded me

of the wisdom and knowledge of plants and secrets of the jungle that she had given me, and I wondered whether I would in turn pass them on to somebody one day. My mother begged me not to leave, and I knew that it would be forever. Tingo Maria was all I had ever known, and as the time of our departure grew nearer I became hysterical with grief, howling and trembling and threatening to kill myself. But there was no time for sentimental indulgence, and I was given sedatives to deal with it.

After the fifth day Gabriel's plans were ready to be carried out. He had booked us flights as it was unsafe for us to be in Tingo Maria any longer.

At the dead of night, he buried one thousand kilos of base cocaine under my parents' house. He of course would not tell me this for several years, knowing that more hysteria would ensue over the prospect of my parents being incriminated as producers. At this stage he felt he had little choice – the rival gangs wanted him dead or alive, and all evidence had to be disposed of without further delay. The merchandise was carried on the backs of several mules, from the production point to my parents' (whose guard dogs were duly bribed with a couple of juicy steaks) and the rest was just a matter of digging a big hole. Sedated with powerful antidepressants, I slept through the whole operation.

The next morning, we woke early and stumbled to the tiny Tingo Maria airport for our flight to Lima. It was the first time

I was leaving my town, my family and my world. Numb with chemicals, apprehensive and homeless, I gripped Gabriel's hand, as our small biplane swirled into the cloudy jungle skies.

Down below, the Huallaga river snaked like a silver thread across the endless green canopy of my beloved jungle. I remembered the legend of the Inca princess who, in her haste to escape an unwanted suitor, dropped her cape which turned into the forest, and her mirror which turned into a lake. From this height it looked as though that might have been the case. I thought of the Sachamama boa and wondered in which part of the river she might be hiding. She had never been able to catch me – but instead it was the curse of cocaine that was forcing me to escape everything I knew. I was a runaway. What was to become of me?

Part 2 – Rosa's Story

Karamandunga

(Sweet Aniseed Buns)

-I-

The first thing that hits you when you arrive in Lima is the smell of damp cloth and rotten fish, a dank mustiness that lingers over everything. It seeps into your skin and clothes, then it enters your home and soaks into your belongings and your soul. If you are not careful, green mould begins to grow, creeping across unused furniture and spreading over walls like a veil. Nature claims her space back.

The mould is a surprise to people when they first settle in Lima – the city crouches, low-rise and sprawling, across a vast expanse of arid desert sand. No other vegetation grows there as it never rains. Only the rich living downtown can afford to buy water and grow bushes and trees in their gardens. Water is a luxury bought by the litre. The poor make do with a plastic container dumped outside their houses, buying from a dubious water truck once a week. Poor people drink contaminated water which smells rancid and swells their children's bellies with parasites.

The lack of vegetation and rain in Lima came as a shock to me when I first moved here, but I am used to it all now. I've been here for ten years and the southern district of Lima, and its "young villages" as the human settlements are known, have become my home. When we arrived, my partner Emanuel and I, Lima was swelling like an abscess, ready to burst with people escaping terrorism and violence and desperate for a better life. I too had come here to put the past behind me. I had seen the glamorous city women in the Venezuelan soap operas on TV, with their lipstick and their tantrums and their large houses full of maids. And I had thought: "One day, that will be me."

But a very different reality awaited. The northern and southern districts of the city, a dust bowl stretching infinitely across sandy hills and rocks, had in those days turned into sprawling slums. A steady influx of people settled there fast, and wherever they could – with the scarce belongings they had brought with them when they fled the countryside.

Ten years ago we had got off a bus after five days' travel from our village in the jungle, exhausted and filthy, still dazed from the tragedy that had forced us to escape, and yearning for a place to rest our weary heads. But we had nothing, and we knew nobody, and we had never seen a city before, let alone one so crowded and dirty as Lima. The bus depot where we were dropped off was in the town centre, in a dilapidated street full of beggars and pickpockets amongst peeling colonial houses with broken, splintered balconies from a bygone era. We had never seen so much grime and human misery, and we had no idea where to go or what to do.

Having asked around near the depot we were told that new arrivals to the capital tended to seek land to settle on in one of the slums, and that we should get a minibus as far north or south as we could manage. Finding an empty plot of land would be more likely there. We stood on the corner of the street as dozens of colourful striped minibuses rattled by, each with a young lad hanging out of the door touting for business by yelling its destination. Having no idea which one to get, we took potluck and found ourselves in a rusty overcrowded people carrier – salsa music blaring and effigies of the Madonna hanging from the rear-view mirror. The minibus wound its way across the dusty city at top speed, until we were the only passengers left and the driver gruffly ordered us off at the last stop.

Waving a stone to ward off the packs of rabid dogs that roamed freely, we cautiously made our way around. We walked past hut after makeshift hut assembled from sheets of straw matting on the sand. There was no water, electricity, or tarmac. Thirsty flies buzzed around dirty patches on the sand, where people had thrown their sewage directly onto the parched ground. The slum dwellers stared cautiously at us as we picked our way clumsily through the deep sand. Neither of us had ever been shy, and we waved and greeted everyone as we tripped through the neighbourhood, eyeing up our surroundings in search of some free space. By this point we were so tired that our heads were spinning, and a few people took pity on us, inviting us into their tiny rickety homes for some coca leaf tea and a plate of hot food.

Many people's stories were like ours – their families had died, or the violence had been approaching their villages leaving them with no choice but to flee. They saw we had arrived with nothing and took us in for a couple of nights.

"We'll lend you some money and tomorrow you can buy some sheets of matting from the market and some rope, and pots and pans. That's what we did when we arrived a few months ago. It's difficult but you will be alright, and everyone helps each other out here," they said.

Eventually, we found an empty plot to settle on, unclaimed and unpopular as it was halfway up a sand hill. The water truck did not stop there, so we would have to carry jerrycans up and down the hill to meet our basic needs. We started with four sheets of straw matting tied together and called it home. The uneven ground sent our belongings toppling and the constant wind rolled the sand from under us, dragging our walls with it. But we were young, and we did not fear discomfort. Our city dream lay ahead and we set about building a life for ourselves.

To survive, crafting was the only option. I soon befriended our neighbours and asked them to teach me the ropes, and to tell me how to find work. They reassured me that jobs were abundant, if tough – all women worked as maids for the wealthy middle-class in the city centre. "These rich people are lazy and they don't even look after their own children. A family will often take on one or two maids to cook, clean and look after them," they explained. "But it's six days a week and you have to sleep there. You'll get a hundred dollars and food." It seemed measly but it was a start.

Emanuel and I had grown up in the same remote village in the Pichis Valley of the Amazon, and even when we were young we knew that we wanted the same things. "Let's go to the big city and get rich," we mused. "That's what everyone else does."

Ours had been a happy, peaceful life, or so it had seemed – although trouble must have been brewing years before the tragedy struck. Our village was very remote and had only fifty people. We all lived in houses on stilts and slept in hammocks at night. Our parents lived from hunting and fishing caimans in the river, and we grew manioc and green bananas.

Emanuel had a cunning glimmer in his eye and was always seeking out opportunities. As a child, he would run errands for neighbours, scuttling as fast as his bare feet would carry him to fetch salt or buy lemons. He could climb trees as fast and as nimbly as a monkey to reach chunks of elusive wild honeycomb, which fetched a handsome price at the village market. His ambition knew no end and he had an eye for a bargain, buying and selling anything he could lay his hands on, from brightly coloured scarves to second-hand radios. I loved his energy and his eye for a good deal and we had been inseparable as children, then as teenagers dreaming together of the silver path of fortune that lay ahead of us.

When we were both nineteen, all the men from our village were massacred by the Shining Path. It seemed that one of our community leaders had openly opposed the communist movement, and a few weeks later the guerrilla troops moved in and shot down all the men on the spot for treason. When they ran out of bullets, the communists drowned everyone else in the river to save time and ammunition. We heard later that the women were taken as slaves and the children were forced to take up weapons and join the movement.

Miraculously, Emanuel and I were spared, as we were out in the forest together at the time, looking for wild honeycomb. We returned after the guerrilla had left and encountered a scene of complete devastation, which fills most of my sleep with nightmares and will haunt me until the day I die. We fled with just the clothes on our backs, crying desperately as we ran to the nearby town, then catching the first bus to Lima.

In those days massacres by the communists were still rare, and the Pichis Valley murders were amongst their first organised killings, aimed at giving out a strong warning to the rest of the country that the Shining Path was not to be reckoned with. Its structures had started to grow more complex and its leadership less tolerant. From a group of idealists, it was now clearly turning into a military operation sending its troops out to quash any rebellion with chilling ruthlessness.

Even now, the heat and glare of Lima's slums could not dim the glimmer in Emanuel's eye. In fact, what had happened to our families had left him even more determined to make a success of this new life.

"You have to start at the bottom of the pile. Don't worry, I have ideas," he chuckled.

When they got to the city, all the women became maids, and all the men ended up driving taxis or working as security guards. Emanuel soon found a job. He spent sixteen hours a day in a small wooden cabin on a middle class, residential street, blowing a whistle every hour to show that he was awake, and to make people feel safe in their homes. He complained about the boredom but used the time well – making friends and contacts in these more commercial parts of the city and building up a network which he would use later.

And so, I became a maid. A neighbour was working for a wealthy family in the leafy Miraflores district of the city and introduced me to a "Senora" – the lady of the house – so that she could vet my credentials. It wasn't long before I was given pink overalls to wear and set to work at the Sanchez family home.

"You must be available to tend to our needs at any time," Senora Sanchez explained in her pristine Lima accent, scrutinising me across her gleaming living room and glancing at her perfectly manicured nails. "Your meals will be our leftovers from the day before. You will eat them in a separate room and use your own toilet and washroom."

I was shocked by this, but grateful to be alive and to have a job, so I set about my work with the enthusiasm and cheerfulness that characterises us jungle folk. The Senora was too rich for her own good, and sat around the house bored, criticising my work and eating sweet aniseed buns called karamandungas.

"You can make me eat from a separate plate if you like – I know who I am and I am slimmer and more beautiful than you," I told her in my head, as I flew around her immaculate home with a duster and mop. I made a point of painting my nails and appearing immaculately turned out for work every day. My dignity was untouched and my jungle spirit untameable by these rich city types.

Senora Sanchez was desperate to keep her home shiny and to protect it from the dust and filth of the outside world. But the outside world always found its way in, much to my secret amusement. Lima was infested with giant, blood-red cockroaches which scuttled noisily into the house and hid in corners. During mating season, they grew wings to go after their love interests and they would tear through the air, heading clumsily but deliberately towards Senora Sanchez.

"Get them off me!" she would scream hysterically – but she was terrified of killing them as it was said that the smell of their corpses would attract many more of them into the house. Much to my disappointment the flying cockroaches did not live long, and the following morning I would find them in the Sanchez family's sun-baked courtyard, dying with their legs in the air.

As hundreds of thousands of people flooded into the city to escape terror in the countryside – or to seek their fortunes – the slums continued to swell, turning the desert sands into a mass of humanity. The government, embroiled in its own corruption scandals, looked on helplessly as the land invasions took place, and people organised themselves into communities, then into neighbourhoods.

Occasionally, an aggressive-looking individual would appear, waving some official looking documents, claiming to be the landlord whose plot was being unlawfully used, and demanding to be paid without delay. After a couple of such visits (often by different but similarly menacing individuals, all making the same claim), a gang of fierce men armed with dogs and guns would follow at the dead of night to scare the living daylights out of the community. Some would crack and move on, but we stayed put – it was rumoured that the next step would be sending bulldozers to mow our huts down like packs of cards, but this rarely happened. People were worried about losing their land, but most had already lost everything once, when they fled the countryside, so they shrugged their shoulders and carried on.

Our jobs meant that Emanuel and I spent very little time in our sandy home in the slums, and the rare nights we had together were precious. After a couple of years, I became pregnant and, as I swelled to enormous proportions, it soon became clear that I was expecting twins. My employer was not impressed, as my belly got in the way of the duster and affected the gleam of her floors, so I was soon dispatched without a severance. But we always fell on our feet, and I resorted to raising funds to continue building our humble home by selling fried chicken to the local community.

Our twins Rosita and Roxana were born extraordinarily pale in complexion, and a year later our son Jaime came along, delicate and effeminate from birth. We tied bright red ladybird seeds around the babies' wrists, as was the tradition to ward off the bad spirits and keep them safe from harm. When the twins first came along Emanuel suspected that I had had an affair with one of the gringos in the American embassy, but I blamed their ghostly complexions on the fright I had one night during my late pregnancy.

I had been trudging along the road on my way back to the slum from Senora Sanchez' house after a long week of work, several months pregnant but still in her service. Night had fallen at 6 o'clock, as it did every single day of the year. I had just got off the bus at the last stop, which was still miles away from home. I hated this walk – the dirt streets were dimly lit, and dogs snarled in the darkness as they crossed my path. Groups of men huddled around bottles of beer in dim corners would cackle and sneer as I scuttled past. The sooner I could get home the better, and I was about halfway when the explosion happened.

I remember a white light and a brute force pulling me backwards to the ground, then screams and pitch darkness. I lay still, shaken but unharmed as far as I could tell, then scrambled to my feet and stumbled towards the flicker of someone's lighter. Around me people began to light fires and attempted to make sense of the damage. Eventually someone explained what was going on. "It's the terrorists. They've blown up the pylons down the road."

The poorer areas were where the electricity pylons were usually erected, and the guerrillas periodically took down the power system with dynamite to drive the city into chaos and bring it to a standstill. It worked, and we certainly suffered from it, but I couldn't help but think that they were targeting the wrong people. The rich would probably switch on their own personal generators and fill their secure houses with comforting light, whilst we were forced into darkness and fear. When the lights went out, Shining Path sometimes lit torches in the shape of a giant hammer and sickle in the mountains above Lima.

Our life in the slums was also punctuated with disease

because of the filthy water we had to buy from the dubious distribution trucks. I would boil my water religiously and cover it with a clean cloth to keep off the flies, but many of my neighbours would simply cross themselves before every drink or meal, entrusting the good Lord with their family's health and fortune. Many succumbed to cholera in those days. The outbreaks would rage in the slums for weeks before the authorities deployed a handful of nervous health workers to investigate what was consuming us all.

One of our neighbours fell victim to the cholera at that time, and it was at her vigil that I discovered that I could access the memories of the dead. As was the tradition, we had been watching over the body all night, drinking fire water by the flicker of a dim strip light. People shuffled in and out throughout the night, paying their respects and munching on coca leaves to stay awake. They slouched on plastic chairs around the room, while the deceased lay on the dining room table in the centre, her rough wooden coffin lined with pink satin and lilies. Occasionally a howl of grief would rise from one or another of our neighbours, or a cough and a sputter, or a loud snore, would punctuate the vigil.

As dawn approached, the women began to heat large vats of chicken broth, its comforting smell wafting through the room like a warm hug. I got up, preparing to leave for work, and placed my hand over our dead neighbour's shoulder to say my goodbyes. Some of her memories flooded through my mind – a wedding, a small child's first steps, hugging an elderly parent and cutting up a sweet mango. Somewhat startled by these unexpected apparitions but floating on the effect of the fire water and lack of sleep, I smiled to myself and to my departed neighbour, and went on my way, thinking little of this newly discovered power.

Life in the slums was harsh. When we were not being driven off our tiny plots of land or succumbing to insanitary diseases, we were shaken by tremors and earthquakes that would drive us from our beds in the middle of the night. If you had recently arrived in Lima and your house was still made of straw matting, it would flop over like cardboard. But if you had saved up and managed to build brick walls, the danger was much greater. There were setbacks and dangers and fear, but people had each other, and the children kept us all going. Our three little terrors, with their smiles and gurgles, helped us put up with the heat and the flies, and we would keep boiling the water, scrubbing them clean and wrapping them in a cocoon of hard work and love.

"We may be poor, but we are never going to be wretched," I would tell the children repeatedly. They were close together in age, and all three were as mischievous as each other. The twins had inherited my jungle cheeriness and marched around singing and dancing, fascinating all the neighbours with their mysterious paleness. And my youngest, Jaime, had the uncanny ability to lead them astray from the youngest age. One day he told them that women become beautiful by spreading raw chillies on their faces, leading to unfortunate face and eye burns and a trip to the emergency department. Another incident involved the three urchins jumping together into the cesspit and having to be rescued, scrubbed and duly vaccinated against the tetanus.

Emanuel gave up his job as a security guard after a couple of years. He said he had made some useful contacts in the city, and they wanted him to supply them with wood from the jungle. No trees grew in Lima's desert sands, and wood was at a premium if you knew how to get hold of it. But I was anxious about Emanuel going back to the jungle in the aftermath of the massacre, and our children were still very young. So he put his plans on hold for a while and sold everything else he could lay his hands on, from kerosene lamps to clothes and TV sets brought over on the bus from Chile, where they could be acquired at lower prices. "Poverty never stopped anyone from wanting a telly," he chuckled, staggering under the weight of four TVs after a seventy-two-hour bus journey to the Chilean border and back.

As the years went by, the slums also became more organised. Rudimentary roads were laid, streets were given names, electricity pylons went up and streetlights began to appear – funded mainly by people selling an abundance of fried chicken to each other. As the authorities had left us to our own devices, we crafted our own solutions, pulling electricity cables from neighbouring areas to supply our houses, running soup kitchens to feed the poorest, scrubbing our children and burying our dead.

The holy church did not miss a trick, and there were many thousands of souls to be saved, so the only proper construction in our slum was the huge Catholic church on the hill – a monolith of concrete crowned with colourful stained glass and a vast bell to summon us all to Mass. An army of nuns descended from Spain and rolled up their sleeves to provide our children with dental care, and our husbands with educational talks about the perils of alcohol. The nuns were dedicated and caring – if a little strict. They would sing their songs and recite their rosaries until we all nodded off in the heat. In due course, the children prepared for first communion, made giddy by the smell of burning incense and excited by the prospect of wearing crisp white dresses.

During Holy Week, the statue of Christ on the cross would be carried through the streets on an ornate silver litter. Red flower petals symbolising His blood, were scattered in its path and hundreds of slum dwellers would join the procession along with civic leaders, priests, nuns and military men.

But despite our love for pomp and ceremony, many of us turned away from the big Catholic church to the other religion – the one being preached by American missionaries in smart suits. They arrived a few years after the Spanish nuns, strummed their guitars, gave the children toys, and talked about hell fire and damnation. They kept our children out of mischief, and with their twangy American accents they were far more entertaining than the Catholics.

-2-

It was at one of the Americans' meetings that I met Maria. She was from the jungle too and we immediately felt like kindred spirits. Like me she had dark, smooth olive skin and coffee coloured eyes and she laughed at everything and waved her arms around when she spoke, as us jungle folk do. We reminisced about life back home, the smells and noises, the plants and the sorcery, and how the fruits used to fall off the trees into our laps. She said very little about what had brought her to Lima, but I imagined she had escaped poverty or violence, or both – just as everyone else had. Maria said her life had been turned around by the faith the Americans preached about. She had discovered a loving God who had forgiven her past mistakes and loved her for who she was. She never told me what her mistakes were, and I did not think of asking her – we were all haunted by dark secrets and tragedies.

I saw Maria at the following meeting organised by the Americans – a Bible study as they called it, which involved very little study and a lot of very dramatic preaching from an American with a loud nasal voice and terrible Spanish. We sat on small rickety wooden benches under a large blue tarpaulin tent donated by American scouts. The tarpaulin was old and full of holes, but for us a precious commodity which sheltered us from the dust and noise of the slum. In winter, its sagging roof also kept away the dreaded garua, the cold sea mist which descended onto the city like a wet cloak.

Maria had brought me a custard apple, which we had traditionally eaten back in the Amazon. "It doesn't taste as good in Lima," she apologised, but we sat together in the dusty makeshift church, wrapped up in childhood memories as the sweet juice dripped off our fingers into the sand. The Americans looked on sternly and encouraged us to return to our Bibles, lest we lose our way in the pleasures of the flesh, so we wiped our sticky hands on our shirts and absent-mindedly got on with our reading.

"You should come along to a Glass of Milk Committee," Maria invited me. "If you help out you get free milk for your family. Apparently, they've already given away a million glasses of milk to hungry kids across the city, and there are new committees being set up every day."

I was keen to get involved. Under the plight of terrorism things were getting worse every day and some of the children in our neighbourhood looked gaunt and starved, roaming the streets like half-wild animals. I had taken some of them home, sat them at my table alongside the twins and Jaime, and given them a bowl of soup and a scrub. But there were too many of them and however many you helped, more would appear the next day, runny-nosed and ravenous.

At the Glass of Milk committee Maria and I would heat huge pans of milk, mix in oatmeal and sugar and watch the little ones pour the warm slop down their throats with enthusiasm. The committee drew women from far and wide, and the milk would always run out before the last child had been fed. But for the volunteers who had got up before dawn to get the wood fire burning and scour the enormous pans ready for heating, there was always enough milk set aside to take home.

"Some say the government is behind the Glass of Milk, but supposing it's the terrorists and they use it to recruit us?" Maria pondered one day, stirring the pan while I blew on the fire.

"No, the milk definitely comes from the government," another mother chipped in – Concepcion, a large lady from the Andes who had never missed a single committee meeting. "And in fact they're threatening to stop the Glass of Milk with all the cuts they're making. Some mothers from the El Augustino committee in the north of town are planning a march on the main square soon. Shall we join them and tell the government they can't put a stop to this, or the children will starve?"

Maria and I looked at each other. The prospect of going to the main square of Lima at this time, when car bombs had been exploding and random shootings were part of the daily news, filled us with dread.

"It's dangerous, but the children need their milk," Concepcion reminded us in her matter-of-fact way.

So off we went, without telling our husbands, who would surely forbid such a trip and hoping that we would all be back by lunchtime to collect the children from school. The previous night, word had reached us from El Augustino that we should bring banners, and that we should all be prepared to demand our basic rights.

"Don't kill, neither with hunger nor with bullets" the banners were to proclaim.

"What if the police think we're communists, will they shoot us?" several women worried. "And what if the Shining Path lines us up and shoots us when we get back home?"

But we gathered our courage and worked through the night painting old sheets and nailing them to scraps of wood. In the morning we were ready to march. We felt emboldened by our banners and by the prospect of having a good shout at the authorities. "Plus, we don't get out much," Maria joked.

We made it to the main square after a long, jolty bus ride across the slums. As we unfolded our banners, we saw women

PART 2 – ROSA'S STORY

flooding towards us from all sides of the square. You could tell they were all poor like us, and many wore the traditional Andean dress, their long braids streaming behind them and their wide skirts bobbing as they marched. We all carried the same message as we walked slowly across the dilapidated city centre, claiming our children's basic right to food, and shunning the violence around us.

There were many more marches after that, and funding for the Glass of Milk continued. In fact, we were told by Concepcion (who always seemed remarkably well informed and attended every march without fail) that it had grown to 5000 committees across the slums and was now considered a political force to be reckoned with. Maria joined Concepcion on the committee and soon began to lead the group – with her feisty jungle spirit and her courage, she had quickly gained the other women's respect.

A few weeks after the march, a comrade from the local Communist Party visited the Glass of Milk committee, offering to come and give a talk to all the mothers. He exhorted us to think about the power of the people and of the uprising we could start during our daily breakfasts. "The time has come to use your voices and to rise against this oppressive government."

But Maria sent him packing. "We are here to feed children, not to do politics for any side," she shouted at him from the other end of a long queue of hungry infants. "And step out of my queue. Only mothers and children are allowed the porridge." The comrade retreated, fuming but looking rather sheepish.

As the years went by, Maria and I kept ourselves busy attending the Americans' meetings and the Glass of Milk committee. The Americans' religion had proved more entertaining than dour Catholicism, and it offered the promise of greater wealth if you attended all the meetings. Its appeal had spread far and wide and the Catholic churches now stood nearly empty. The Glass of Milk committee grew into quite a national institution. Our branch was visited frequently by scared-looking academics from Lima's top universities, who asked us questions and scribbled down our answers, then wrote wordy papers about how people at the grassroots were resisting the influence of the Shining Path.

Over time, Maria also became quite a focus of attention as she spoke up against the Communists and their recruitment methods. Inspired by her faith, and by Concepcion and the march on Lima, she began to organise all the mothers in the community into groups. "Let's find ways to survive the crisis in our country," she would say, and began expanding the Glass of Milk committee's activities to provide hot meals for the poor. She brought people in to give talks while we ate, and they told us about our fundamental human rights. She started producing colourfully illustrated pamphlets about these, and there was always a petition going round highlighting injustice or abuse which she would bring to the district authorities.

"If we are strong enough to defend others then we should," Maria would say.

In the community we all supported each other, and I slowly built a home for my family. After a while I was able to replace our straw matting walls with wood, and then to save up for bricks and mortar. One fine day, Emanuel and I poured a layer of cement over the sand and we finally had a washable floor. I proudly polished it every single day using gasoline, which provided extra shine and a heady aroma.

Emanuel did not spend much time admiring my freshly cleaned floors as he was frequently away. By this point I had given in and let him become a wood tradesman, and he brought logs from deep inside the rainforest to be sold in the city. I was never really sure where the wood came from, nor how he got hold of it, but he made a good living from it and we were slowly able to furnish our house and buy the children school uniforms and good shoes.

"Cedarwood" was all he told me with that irresistible twinkle in his eye, as he returned home after his long logging trips, the pungent smell of sweet bark clinging to his clothes.

But I had heard that it was a dangerous business. Buying the wood was mostly illegal and he then had to float it down the river for many miles, facing the beasts and dangers of the Amazon waterways. Luckily, he never travelled alone – he had several associates, as he called them, who travelled together to these remote parts. They negotiated together, braving the dangers and discomfort together and dividing out the earnings once the precious wood had reached the log buyers in the city's sawmills.

After one particularly fruitful trip, Emanuel returned home with three of his associates, bearing celebratory gifts of smoked pork and rice wrapped in banana leaves, and a few crates of cold beer.

All three associates were Mexican, colourful, and loud. I laughed at their bad jokes and at their moustaches, but in reality I found them quite intimidating. They lay around our house all day smoking and drinking beer, their muddy jungle boots strewn all over my pristine, gasoline-polished floors. They swore profusely and used big words to belittle us Peruvians and to proclaim the might and superiority of Mexico.

Their leader Miguel was the most outspoken. As well as being broad and stocky he also had the biggest moustache. "Look at this place," he scorned. "You are all living on top of each other, in abject poverty. Flies everywhere. All barely scraping by and piled up in these godforsaken slums. Don't you want a better life, don't you aspire to bigger things?"

I was a proud woman and soon put him in his place with a couple of insults about his manners and witty comments about his moustache. But deep down I knew he was right.

Years of fear and violence had left us crushed and had snuffed out our ambition.

"So, what do you suggest, Miguel?" I enquired defensively, hands on hips to show I wasn't all that pleased with the way he was thanking me for my hospitality.

"What you need is a big business idea. The wood we buy is good, and people will want it in Mexico. We can ship it there instead of getting such a low price selling it to the sawmills here in Lima. I know people, I can connect you to them."

I scoffed the idea away and ordered Miguel to pick up his boots and to make himself useful while he was staying under my roof. But the seed had been sown.

The Mexicans stayed at our house for several months. They said it was a particularly bad rainy season in the jungle that year, and that they had to wait before they could go back for more wood. Emanuel seemed to enjoy their company and they played with the children when I had to go out, so I put up with them and smiled as they lay around drinking beers and making grand plans for my family's future.

"All you need to do is register as a business and we will help you with the paperwork and all the rest. You can finally make real money and finish building your house and put your children into good schools."

Our children were bright and being able to give them the best education was a dream I had always considered out of reach. I captured these thoughts and pieced them together in my mind like a colourful patchwork sewn with silver thread. A better future for the next generation was the dream of every mother.

In the end I gave in and we set to work, grappling with the intricacies of the Peruvian bureaucratic system. Forms were filled in and registration numbers filed, notaries contracted, and invoice books printed. Finally the day came: the business was set up and, by some small miracle considering the unfortunate rain season we had suffered, a large number of logs arrived by lorry to Lima's port of Callao. The Mexicans had provided the working capital needed for their purchase, and diligently transferred the precious logs to a shipping container bound for the Mexican port of Manzanillo.

The day before the container was due to depart, I found myself signing a pile of forms – they were full of long words and endless clauses but seemed to be about my responsibility for content and shipment between both ports. It was an exhilarating feeling to be a businesswoman and to be making my first overseas dispatch.

I completed and handed over the papers before retiring home late that evening, content and relieved that the shipment was finally ready. Surely soon I would receive a handsome sum of money into my bank account from the Mexican wood buyers, and I would start investigating the best private schools in the area for the twins.

But the next morning, I was awoken just before dawn by a loud hammering on the front door. Staggering to answer it, I was met by two armed policemen. Parked on the sand track was their vehicle, shiny and black with bullet proof windows.

"Are you responsible for the shipment of thirty tons of wood towards the port of Manzanillo in Mexico?" they barked loudly, brandishing a carbon copy of the document I had filled in the night before.

"What is wrong? The wood was good, and it came with certificates of origin. All the paperwork had been completed."

"Yes, the wood was fine," the officer explained. "The problem is that the shipment was searched last night – a routine check. Packed inside the wood there were two hundred kilos of cocaine base. I don't know if you were responsible or if you have been tricked, but you are under immediate arrest. Please come with us."

A few simple words are all it takes to tear someone's life apart. I swayed like a scarecrow and the earth seemed to give way under me, but I followed the men without putting up a fight. Emanuel was away at the time and the Mexicans were nowhere to be seen. I called Concepcion and entrusted her with my children who were still fast asleep, blissfully unaware. She threw up her hands and cried in distress, promising me this was just a terrible mistake and that she would alert Maria and all the other mothers from the Glass of Milk Committee to back me up. There was no lawyer, no process, no explanation and, for the time being, no trial. That morning I went straight from my happy family home in the sandy slums to Santa Monica, Lima's only prison for women.

I will never forget the moment I arrived at the prison gates and entered the compound, numb with shock and sick with fear after an hour-long drive in the back of the police van. I was bundled out, searched, given prison scrubs and a prison number then taken to the cell I would be sleeping in.

I had heard horror stories about the men's prison in Lima, but Santa Monica wasn't that bad. With its brightly painted walls it could first be mistaken for a school, but a closer look revealed barbed wire and security cameras above the walls. We slept in tiny cells which we shared with one other woman. These confined living quarters soon filled up with posters of film stars, heart-shaped decorations from loved ones and other reminders of the outside world.

Santa Monica was full of terrorists, thieves and unfortunate foreign women who had been caught acting as drug mules. My Peruvian inmates could not understand how these young girls had got themselves in such an unfortunate position. "Surely they didn't get into that trade willingly, knowing that they risked ending up here" we all wondered as we watched them, tall and striking, tearing their blonde hair out with despair as they paced across the prison patio.

Most of the inmates were like me, dazed and bewildered after having been tricked or manipulated in some way – or so they all said – and we supported each other and soon formed strong friendships. We also learnt to earn our keep – the prison favoured keeping the inmates busy and training them up to go back to an honest life on release. The prison put on endless classes where crafts, cookery and other skills were taught every day. The prison patio was a thriving marketplace full of delicious food smells, when it wasn't the scene of daily aerobics classes.

I kept strong by day, busily filling the hours, and learning skills I could use as soon as I was released. But the nights were long. Until this moment in my life, I had always believed that we can control our own destiny and be free, but once I was inside those prison walls, I looked back at my life and feared that a curse had doomed my family to tragedy. Every night I prayed to the Virgin Mary, to Saint Martin the saint of the poor and the oppressed, and to the God of the noisy American missionaries. I begged for justice and I cried for revenge. But for months nothing happened, and the Mexicans were never heard of again.

Emanuel would visit me every week with a look of complete despair in his eyes. He implored me for forgiveness and beat his chest with rage, vowing to kill the Mexicans with his bare hands if ever he came across them again. He was trying to get me a good lawyer, but these kinds of cases were common, and the cost of legal support was beyond our reach. He was managing to stay on top of things, though, and we discussed at length whether he should bring the children in to visit me, or whether it was better to protect them from the truth.

At night and under the influence of my despair, I started walking through the prison walls and wandering back home to hug my children. In another dream an angel came to me and told me that there was another life ahead, that there was still hope and that all was not lost.

Because of the ability I had to access the memories of the dead, I began using the idle hours in prison to wander around other women's pasts. I especially visited the past lives of murder victims, of those who had been killed by the murderers now serving term in Santa Monica. One woman came to my thoughts often. Although she was not in the prison, I knew that she was responsible for many women's deaths. Her name was Augusta and she was a powerful terrorist. She carried many stories and a trail of memories from the people she had killed. These filled my nights, the happiness of their earlier lives and families mixing with the screams and horror of their dying moments.

Part 3 – Augusta's Story

Jalatoro

(Bull Run)

-I-

I was born in Huanta, near the mountain city of Ayacucho, where two hundred and fifty years earlier our ancestors fought a major battle of independence against the Spanish conquest. Nestled in the central highlands, ours was a proud, ancient city full of bustle and commerce. Steep cobbled streets rose towards the bright blue Andean skies, and ancient Spanish churches stood at every street corner. Market stalls filled the air with smells and shouts and farmers flocked into town to peddle colourful vegetables and grains laden on the backs of weary looking llamas. Old women stirred pans of hot herbal drinks which they served steaming in gourds, and mountains of aniseed and cinnamon bread towered in cloth covered baskets.

Ours was a traditional mountain life. My mother looked like a painting and wore the pollera, the big billowy skirts of the Andean women; a hundred petticoats rustling as she walked. My parents sang gentle Quechua lullabies to me and my sister Gisela, as they bounced us on their knees. "Punulla Waway, just sleep my child, just sleep" they sang, until we nodded off, wrapped in rough llama wool blankets, cheeks flushed from the fresh air of the altitudes.

"Just sleep my child, just sleep
Just rest my child, just rest
I must go to work the earth
The spirit must come my child
"Come with me" he has to say
With whom I'm going to talk, I do not know
With whom I'm going to laugh, I do not know
Where I will find you, I do not know
My child with whom I laugh
My child with whom I play."

But as soon as we were old enough to understand the words of the lullaby, my parents told us about poverty and the long suffering of our people as they worked the land. They said that the oppression we endured was all down to the behaviour of the rich and powerful who ruled over our country.

"The government will always keep the people in submission and poverty," my father said. "They have never cared about us and they never will, and that is why we all need to prepare for a revolution."

As well as being a child of the Andes, I was born into Communism. My father was a Party militant and my grandfather was a prominent political figure in the province.

My grandparents had experienced the poverty and grind of work in the nearby copper and silver mines, which were owned by the British imperialists. My grandfather had joined the Party, together with his fellow miners, as a reaction to the exploitation and appalling conditions all the workers endured. My parents were slightly better off as they had gained an education and had both become primary school teachers, but their loyalty to the Party was just as strong.

All around me growing up, there were hammers and sickles and red flags and pamphlets. Gatherings took place in our house and people would file in quietly then sit together for hours to discuss the state of the nation and the class struggles. The Andean resistance was on the rise, and it was starting in our small front room.

The People had been forgotten for too long, my parents' visitors said. But we had learnt from our Chinese and Russian brothers, far away in those barren, frozen parts of the world we could barely imagine existed. We had learnt that an uprising was the only possible solution.

My father was a great storyteller and before bedtime every night, by the flicker of the bedside candle, he would tuck me into my cot as the cold drew in from the mountain peaks. He would tell me and Gisela all about the military strategies of Uncle Mao, the ideology of Uncle Lenin and the authority of Uncle Stalin. I listened with wide eyes, my young heart pounding with excitement. I struggled to find sleep after hearing about the achievements of our brave comrades overseas, and I wished I could grow up fast to become just like them.

When he was not dreaming of a brighter future, my father would take me with him to see the bull run in the centre of the city of Ayacucho. Known locally as the jalatoro, this custom had been introduced during the Spanish conquest and adapted to our local ways. A carnival atmosphere filled the cobbled streets, which were lined with revellers dressed in their Sunday best. The women lit up the streets with their layers of bright, colourful clothing, including capes, shawls, embroidered skirts, and vibrantly coloured hats. The men looked spectacular in their ponchos, their embroidered chumpi belts and their chuspas, decorated pouches used to hold coca leaves.

Once the crowds had downed a few beers and copious amounts of fire water, the bulls were let loose. Bewildered at first, and dazzled by the midday sunlight, they soon began to charge aimlessly down the narrow streets, nostrils flared and flanks foaming, spurred on by the crowds' drunken brawl. The local men would duck and dive, showing off to the women who screamed and whooped. As we watched, my father would tell me about power and weakness and the way out of servitude.

"Look at those bulls. Learn from them. Always fight, never

bow your head," he whispered as he held me close to protect me from the stampede.

My parents taught us well at school, and at home they encouraged us to read avidly about the history of Peru and the Communist manifesto. As I reached my teenage years, the meetings at our house intensified. It became hard to fit everyone into our small adobe dwelling, and the gatherings spilled into the community hall, then graduated to the town hall. Many people were drawn to the communist ideal and its promise of a new life, a new hope for their children.

One of the most frequent attendees was Abimael Guzmán, one of my father's friends from the Party, who taught philosophy at the local university. This learned institution had recently resumed its teaching after being closed for half a century under the succession of military regimes we had endured. Many of Guzmán's students started attending the meetings at our house, saying he had planted the revolutionary seed in their minds during his stirring lectures.

"Marxism–Leninism will open the shining path to revolution," Guzmán announced resolutely at our meetings, where he was nearly always the key speaker. Despite being an academic, he carried himself like a true political leader – his eyes were brazen and his deep voice carried his audience along with him:

"Comrades. Our labour has ended, the armed struggle has

begun. The invincible flames of the revolution will glow, turning to lead and steel. There will be a great rupture and we will be the makers of the new dawn. We will convert the black fire into red and the red into pure light."

Extreme poverty was rife in Ayacucho and the neighbouring regions in those days. Families with six children or more huddled in makeshift mud-floored houses without running water. They scratched at the land for a few potatoes and if they were lucky, a handful of surplus broad beans and a chicken to trade at the market. But mostly they went to bed cold, hungry and sick.

The poor had been abandoned by the state a long time ago, going back to colonial times. Back in the days of the Incas and the Aymaras, our civilisation had centred around the land, and protecting those who respected and cared for it through their arduous work. But for hundreds of years since we had all suffered through ancestral violence, the cruel treatment of the indigenous cultures, the repressive violence of successive military dictatorships and their bad treatment of the peasant people. The ruling classes ignored our suffering. But they also held us under their thumb and stopped us from revolting.

We all had at least one neighbour who had been jailed without trial, condemned to rot in a cell for years before being released inexplicably one day. It was clear to us all that the proletariat needed to rise and restore justice by taking control of Peru, then of the rest of the world. Together we would arrive at full Communism. Together, we would share the fruits of our land – the corn, chillies, potatoes and quinoa provided so abundantly by our mother earth, the Pachamama. The old regime would collapse, and a new state would be born.

Guzmán spoke well and he knew all the right words, but I questioned him often.

"Radical ideology is all very well, but we are just here talking, for hours and hours on end. When are we going to put these theories into practice?"

Clearly this was the most earth-shattering thing the great revolutionary had ever heard. He stared at me for a long time, perhaps finally noticing this quiet young girl who came to all his speeches and sat on the front row at his rallies, her quiet sister by her side.

Years later Guzmán would write to me: "Ayacucho, an afternoon in April ... blue skirt, beige blouse and the beautiful woman emerges from the girl walking at seventeen. And our life together began, love and struggle, growing struggle and deeper love, solid, fertile."

Shortly after this conversation had taken place, Guzmán invited me to be his second in command. At first, I thought he was joking, but he called me Comrade Norah and made me stand next to him during his public speeches. Soon I was running my own events and campaigns which drew growing crowds. I pulled my shoulders back, stood tall and, quoting Karl Marx, urged my comrades to act against the ruling classes. My parents were immensely proud and supportive of my endeavours, and wholeheartedly agreed with my work. At our meetings they would sing the communist songs as loud as their vocal cords would allow them, left hands held to hearts and eyes brimming with fervour.

Then one day when I was nineteen, Guzmán cupped my face with his hands and said, "Beautiful Comrade Norah, you cannot be my second in command in this great fight, without also being my wife." He was much older than me, but age had no role to play in our fight, and I knew he was right. We needed to be an indivisible team, bound together in body and spirit by the greatest forces, if our quest were to succeed.

So, at springtime that year I married Abimael Guzmán, unreservedly giving him – and communism – my body and my mind. I became a staunch and committed comrade. I was ready for wartime.

Instead of going on a honeymoon, Guzmán and I studied communist ideology in more depth by travelling to the People's Republic of China. It was a monumental undertaking to leave the Andes and make our way to the other side of the world. It took us days to reach the port of Callao, then a month on a freight boat to get to China, which was as foreign and desolate to us as the moon. Yet on arrival we were greeted warmly by our Chinese brothers, and their flags and their songs confirmed what we had been dreaming of for so long – that we had found our home-from-home, the motherland of our battle. The language barrier did not hinder our quest, and we spent three happy weeks immersed in the workings of the Party. We learnt all about the command economy and democratic centralism, and we plotted how we would adapt the genius of the Chinese model to transform our beloved Peru.

After returning from China, Guzmán said it was time for him to leave his job as head of personnel for San Cristóbal of Huamanga University. The time had come to put our plans into action and to go underground. With great sadness but knowing this was the only way to pursue our cause, I said goodbye to my beloved parents and tearful sister and followed him into hiding.

Guzmán's followers called him President Gonzalo, the leader of the Shining Path. We plotted our insurgence against the government, using Ayacucho as our base and sending our comrades across the country to spread the word and train up others. The students were our biggest allies. Their intellects embraced the concepts we were preaching, and their hearts were full of youthful fire. They were tasked with spreading the word at universities in other cities and in Lima, to swell the number of comrades in our army, and to prepare for the armed struggle.

Our clandestine meetings in Ayacucho became known as

the Central Committee's second plenary, with the blessing of our Chinese brothers - and we formed a Revolutionary Directorate led by Guzmán. The Directorate ordered its militias to transfer to strategic areas across the provinces to start the struggle.

Despite my political upbringing, there had been no violence in my family. My father was a peaceful man and his anger towards the state had been expressed in words, not through arms. But I knew we needed to go a step further if we were to succeed. Nobody listens to the poor. Even if they learn to use big words they will always be ignored and neglected. Even what felt like a loud clamour to us would not be heard by those in power, from the comfort of their big homes in Lima. Only by attacking what made them feel safe, their precious army and their self-serving economy, would we make them sit up and listen. Our power could only come from the barrel of a gun.

Of course, many would have to die before we could see the ushering-in of the utopian peasant-based regime of pure Marxism-Maoism. Our fight would need to target the army and police, but also government employees, workers who did not participate in the strikes we organized, peasants who cooperated with the government in any way – including by voting in their so-called democratic elections – and the middle-classes in the main cities.

Our plan was clear. First, we would get resources and then

we would get power. In the remotest villages of the Andes we began gathering weapons. They were easy to get hold of, as the peasants had them and were willing to sell them to us in exchange for protection against the narcos and the army. But we went a step further and paid them a higher price for their coca, gradually recruiting the peasants into cells and selling it on to finance our operations.

Several comrades pointed out that we should not fund ourselves alone, and that help ought to be sought from communist insurgency groups in Russia, China, and Cuba, who were wealthier than we were. But Guzmán was adamant that we would make our own way and that the pursuit of money was precisely what was rotting the brains of our enemies. "If you don't have a gun, bring your machetes," he would urge. "Or make your own weapons with whatever you have."

Often, when I was negotiating on the price of weapons in the tiny villages I travelled through, I was the only woman, and my comrades would look at me with contempt and slight horror in their eyes. "This is a war, there is no place in it for women," they would sneer. But I knew that in this battle we would be equal to men, and that we should fight alongside them.

I was twenty-four years old when I established the People's Women movement. At last, after centuries in the dark, I hoped Peruvian women would be able to access education, social justice, and opportunities to act alongside men in the People's War. In the revolution, we decided that women would be treated in the same way as men, and during militant actions we would stand side by side, armed, prepared, and fearless.

It was 1980, and we were coming out of twelve years of military dictatorship. Democracy was a concept so vague and unknown to us that we put it down to imperialist propaganda spread by the Americans, a nation deprived of morality who worshipped their insane new gods: railroads, highways, and cocaine. So we refused to vote and focused on starting our Guerrilla war.

On May 17th, the armed struggle against the government finally began. It was election day – the first one in Peru for twenty-five years – and we launched our first uprising by burning the ballot boxes in Chuschi, a small town in the Ayacucho province. Some of the officials who were handling the ballot boxes in the community buildings tried to oppose us and had to be shot in the offensive. I was saddened by this first killing under my watch, but we had no choice – these people were corrupt government officials and as such, traitors of the people.

On the same day in Lima, the comrades we had recruited from the universities followed our instructions and hung dead dogs in doorways, with slogans from the Chinese revolution painted on placards around their necks. The signs warned that corrupt people would be punished like capitalist dogs. The ripple we had started soon turned into an unstoppable wave, as our actions spread across the country. People had suffered for long enough and were ready to prepare for war. I too knew that this was the right path, and that it was the will of the people that we should lead them unwaveringly in the fight against oppression.

One day soon after this, I led a group of comrades to a village in the Pichis Valley, whose chief was reported to be plotting a rebellion against us. It was just after dawn when we made our way through the dirt path towards the village that morning, on foot to avoid raising the alarm. In the freshness of the morning our boots crunching along the gravel were the only sound around us, as we walked resolutely on our mission.

We were armed with Russian Kalashnikovs and knew the villagers would only have machetes, but we were to follow our orders into this unequal battle. We had a message to show the neighbouring villages what we did to those who opposed us. My comrades and I feared nothing and had learned to be ruthless in the face of opposing forces that sought to squander our quest for the truth.

The chief's house was easy to single out. It was larger than the neighbouring huts and stood on stilts for protection against snakes and other predators. Houses in the area had no walls as there was no electricity and so no need to erect walls for privacy.

We swiftly swung up the makeshift wooden ladder that led to the chief's home. Inside the whole family was assembled for breakfast around the log fire where chicken broth was stewing. The chief leapt up in terror seeing our rifles and immediately started to beg us for mercy, as the rest of the family sat frozen in silence.

"Brothers, we haven't done anything, please spare our children," the chief implored.

"We have come on behalf of the glorious revolution," I announced. "We have heard that you are openly betraying us and working with the imperialist dogs to create an insurgence against us. This has saddened our comrade Guzmán as he thought you were on our side and against the oppressor. He has sent us here to ask why you are turning away from us."

A dog began barking from below the house, raising the alarm.

The chief was holding up his hands and his eyes darted around the room and beyond the hut's platform. I knew now was the time to move, yet my whole body felt heavy as if it weighed a tonne.

"You should do what we say because we know best," I repeated calmly. I nodded to a comrade, Jorge, who opened fire on the chief and his family, in a sharp staccato followed by silence as their bodies shuddered and slumped to the ground.

We ran through the village and shot a few more of their men by means of reinforcing the message. When we ran out of bullets, Jorge and Fito drowned a few others in the river to save time and ammunition. Later they would return to round up the women and children and ensure they joined the movement.

"If we don't kill them, they'll kill us," I reminded the men as we left the village. I knew this was what had to be done, in service to the all-powerful and infallible ideology that illuminated our path and armed our minds. But, as we hastily retreated into the rainforest, the image of my father came to me, holding me close as a child in Ayacucho while the bulls stampeded by, protecting me from danger. I found myself wishing this war would hurry up and get over, that things would get back to normal and that I could walk through a village like this one in peace.

As we marched on, I saw two teenagers coming out of the forest towards the scene of devastation in the village, a girl and a boy with sheer terror in their eyes. I knew I should order the men to shoot them down and finish the job we had started, but I pretended not to see them as we went on our way. To this day I hold the image of these two young people in my mind, carved in the depths of my memory – and I hope that they managed to get away to a new life.

Ten years flew by. The uprising of the poor continued. From our radical student base, we now had swathes of women behind us, as well as the mass segments of the peasant population who had felt overlooked by the state for so long. The fight was strengthened through our cell structure, which had us all organised into strict hierarchy and effectively resisted penetration by our enemies.

I was proud of our appeal to Andean women, building on their dissatisfaction with the patriarchal system. Soon, women made up a high proportion of our membership, and were portrayed as teachers and martyrs in our propaganda images, hair flowing and fists bared. We began holding trials of wife-beaters, adulterers, and rapists. Divorce was introduced into the rural villages and sexual harassment was not tolerated. The shackles that had held women under the oppression of their fathers, their husbands, and the capitalists, were finally being broken.

The President at the time, Alan Garcia, was our first so-called democratic leader. He said democracy had to defend itself, to justify sending the army to stamp us out. But we knew that the government was overwhelmed, and the army was in chaos. It was only succeeding in killing as many civilians as we were, but without achieving our revolutionary goals.

By the early nineties, it seemed possible that the Shining Path's power was entrenched and absolute, and that a military coup was finally in sight. Our campaign was successfully demoralizing and undermining the government, and we had weakened the structures upon which the oppression of the poor had been built. We were creating a new Peru. The Shining Path was now the Vanguard of world communism, and it seems we could rebuild a new life from the ashes.

But I had been striving and fighting for more than ten years and I was tired. Guzmán and I had been working together for all our married life. Our political campaign and the hardship of travelling endlessly across the country, risking death at every turn, had strained our marriage beyond repair. On occasion when we were in the same village or house we would clutch each other tightly, whispering encouraging words before falling into restless, paranoid sleep.

One night, as we lay in bed after an evening of planning with the local militant group, I dared to have a moment of weakness.

"Abimael, I'm exhausted. We've all been living in fear for years. Is it all really worth it?"

Guzmán looked at me darkly and slowly shook his head. "This isn't like you, comrade Norah. What has come over you? Those who join the revolution must never sway. We are bound to our cause and to it we must remain faithful, and steadfast in our belief."

"But so much death, Abimael," I said simply. "Is the glorious revolution really worth so much death?"

Looking back, I think that was the night when Guzmán lost his blind faith in me. He needed those around him to be unswervingly loyal, and his own wife was showing signs of doubt. I was at risk of failing him and of failing our cause.

Our encounters grew less frequent as Guzmán's power base grew. I hardly recognised him anymore and I became suspicious of him and of the younger female comrades and devotees who surrounded him, and with whom he spent increasing amounts of time. His power and charms had turned into a toxic syrup that drew women to him like a Venus flytrap. One of his devotees was a delicate-looking flower called Elena Iparraguirre, also known as Comrade Miriam.

Elena had been a childhood friend of mine in Huanta and she had joined the Party as early as I had done. She was wholly committed to the revolution, ambitious and ruthless, having left behind her husband and three children to follow us in our quest. She had been climbing the ranks in the Party under Guzmán's watchful eye and was currently his third-incommand.

I don't know if it was the growing distance between us that pushed Guzmán towards even greater violence. Shining Path's increasingly brutal methods, together with strictly imposed curfews, the prohibition of alcohol and an overall sense of insecurity and fear led to an increasingly popular reaction against the Communist Party.

People were becoming worn out. They had begun to say that Guzmán looked like a Che Guevara, but that he had become a Pol Pot. We were embroiled in a cyclical state of violence in which Maoist guerrillas embarked in ruthless punitive expeditions against Peruvian civilians living in the Andean region. Thousands of people had now died and whole communities had been decimated in the name of our cause.

The tide was turning. Guzmán's plan to rally the people of the countryside to his side had begun to backfire. Within months the rural militia galvanised growing support for the military against the Shining Path. The very peasants Guzmán had sacrificed himself to defend, had turned against him. We had failed to create the workers' state through an invincible people's war, and now our insurgence was beginning to look like a narco gang.

Whilst my ideological belief in communism and a new world order were still just as strong, I felt distant from what my comrades had become, and I no longer believed in my husband. With a sinking heart, I resolved to run away and to reassess the truth. But as one of the leaders of the Shining Path, this would require me to disappear completely. My only route to doing so was by hiding in the depths of human undergrowth – by immersing myself in dirty, sprawling Lima.

-2-

When I arrived in Lima, finding a way to disappear was my priority. I must not be found by the authorities and my enemies were everywhere. I would be tracked down swiftly wherever I tried to hide and killed as a terrorist traitor. Even in the slums, amongst the millions living on top of each other like ants, I would be smoked out in no time. I would need to go undercover by adopting the most unlikely scenario. With nothing but the clothes on my back, I wandered into a green, leafy square in Comas, one of Lima's middle-class residential areas. Smart houses stood behind gates, protected from the world, and guarded by men in brown uniforms. These were the houses of the working rich, those who owned businesses and had maids, but believed in opportunity, hard work and determination.

Nobody would look for me here, and these people were too busy to read the newspapers or realise who I was. I knocked on a few doors and told the same story each time – I was escaping the violence in Ayacucho and desperate for a roof over my head and a plate of food. Would they let me work for them as a maid? I tried to behave like a typical peasant, shuffling my feet, mumbling in broken Spanish, and avoiding eye contact. In my heart I held my hatred and disdain for their bourgeois privilege.

I was in luck – at the fourth house, a flustered looking housewife answered, hair dishevelled and two toddlers clinging to her legs. She had just fired her latest maid after discovering her stealing from the family savings and was happy to take me on for a trial. I would work six days a week, cooking, cleaning and looking after the children so that she could go back to work. Her name was Marta Ramirez and she and her husband ran an iron soldering business. They crafted solid but ornate gates so that the middle classes could shield themselves with elegance from the violence and grime of the outside world.

I set about my tasks immediately, cleaning the house, cooking for the family and caring for the children – it all seemed easy enough as long as I kept my head down and bided my time until the coast was clear for me to return to the provinces. When Marta asked me about my background, I pretended to be Quechua speaking with limited Spanish, and said simply, "I am from Ayacucho, Senora." I invented a story about how peasant roots and grinding poverty had driven me to find work in the capital, an all too common story which she would have no trouble believing.

At this time, the cities were being shaken by violence too, as the reactionary capitalists were concentrated in the urban areas, defending the metropolis and capitals. Our movement had been rooted in the countryside, in small villages with the masses – especially with the poor peasants. But having harnessed the disorganised force of the peasant people into a powerful army, the time had now come for the Shining Path to target the cities.

Soon after I began living at the Ramirez, we heard about the first bombings in central Lima. There was a wavering in electric power followed by one of the blackouts common in the city at that time. Marta was at home when we heard the distant blast, which we assumed to be coming from the town centre. She screamed and started phoning around in a panic to see if any of their friends and family had been affected. The bombs had gone off in Miraflores, an upmarket business district of the city. Two trucks, each packed with a tonne of home-made explosives, exploded on the street outside the national bank.

It soon transpired that dozens had died or were wounded and in hospital. The bombs had dug a vast crater of destruction affecting hundreds of wealthy homes and businesses. For a week, my companions raged their campaign of violence in the capital, bringing it to near shutdown. This was the first direct attack on a city centre, and the first time during the civil war that members of "traditional", well-off society would be made to feel the conflict. I suspected that my companions would be happy with their work; the time was right to take the fight to the next level, to spread to the city the all-powerful and infallible ideology that illuminated our path and armed our minds.

However in the aftermath of the event, as I scrubbed the floors of the Ramirez house while the family wailed over the friends they had lost in the blast, I wondered whether we had gone too far and if this bloodshed did anything to advance our purpose.

People in the cities have louder voices, and the wake of the incident saw intensified public outrage. This pushed the President to crack down more heavily on our groups. It was best for me to keep my head low, and I decided to spend a considerable amount of time in hiding. I had no contact with Guzmán or with our companions and had told none of them where I was going. There were cells dotted across the slums of Lima, where I knew I could find them when I was ready to return to the fold.

After so many years of living as a revolutionary, in hiding or on the run, life as a maid was a shock to the system – a strange new beginning, away from danger. My days were punctuated by routine and normality; getting up at dawn every morning, preparing breakfasts, getting children up and gently coaxing them to go to school. After this I would buy food at the local market, gradually getting to know the tradesmen and the other maids who went there every day.

People were reserved; most had come from the countryside and were not used to small talk. The other maids were often in a rush to get back to their domestic tasks. But as time went by, I grew to know some of them and learnt about their lives. We exchanged brief conversations whilst choosing cuts of chicken or bags of ground chilli, and I found out that many of the maids were treated as near-slaves by their masters, with no rights and no time off. They worked fourteen hours a day six to seven days a week and sent a scant salary home to their husbands and children, whom they never got to see. They were not allowed to eat with the families they served, nor use the same plates lest they contaminate them. This abject subjugation reminded me why our revolution was so needed.

However, I also grew to realise that I had struck gold with the Ramirez family. From the beginning they treated me with kindness and respect, thanking me for the duties I carried out, seating me at their table for meals, sharing with me their daily worries and family joys. In the evenings they would invite me to sit with them in the living room to sip on a glass of pisco. They discussed politics and I heard for the first time how those of their class thought about the situation in our country.

"I'm not surprised people are unhappy," Marta's husband reflected. "The poverty in the provinces is grinding and those who own the mines just strip the land bare and drive out people who have lived there for centuries. But the Shining Path will achieve nothing. Its leaders are just as corrupt as the government, and its days are numbered. What this country needs is to modernise, to bring in more technology, more foreign investment to create more jobs."

Marta and her husband paid me well and even arranged for me to have private health insurance and a savings account, something I had never heard of before. I knew I was giving in to the evils of capitalism in this new life, and that my comrades would be horrified at my betrayal – but I was strangely drawn to this new feeling of financial comfort. I left the account empty, preferring to stuff the bank notes I received into the recesses of my narrow mattress.

I was invited on family holidays and for barbecues on the outskirts of the city. The children would sit on my knee and ask for stories about the Andes. I could not tell them the truth about my communist past, so I began inventing stories about a village illuminated by bright sun and pure blue skies.

"We grew maize and harvested it at full moon, when we knew the moon goddess, Mama Kilya, would weep her silver tears and make it bountiful."

These stories were made up, but the children loved hearing about this way of living so distant and different to theirs, in a land where people's bond with the soil was still strong, and where the peasants still believed in myths and goddesses.

"Tell us more about the Andes!" they implored, setting me on course for yet another bedtime story.

I told them about the Incas and their gods, and how ruins of their great cities had been found set in a perfect straight line towards the moon. I told them about the peasants and their customs and their lands. I told them about the smell of lemongrass, paico and chuchuhuasi. I even told them about the running of the bulls, and I spoke about power and weakness and servitude. But I didn't tell them about the military strategies of Uncle Mao, the ideology of Uncle Lenin or the authority of Uncle Stalin.

Life started to feel calm and pleasant, punctuated by mundane domestic tasks and family routine. It was difficult not to warm towards those I had seen as the enemy. With time I cautiously began to regard Marta, her husband and their children like my own family. I saw how hard they worked and how much they loved each other. I noted the way they treated me in contrast with the experience of other maids around me. My initial hatred for their class was turning into admiration and a sense of loyalty.

After I had lived with the Ramirez family for two years, my mattress began to feel swollen and lumpy with stashed dollar notes. But I did not have time to get used to sleeping in my bumpy bed – a series of unfortunate events led the Ramirez' iron soldering business to face bankruptcy. This was common at the time – the political instability, bombings and hyperinflation were not the best environment for a small family business. One day, Marta came down to breakfast in tears. She confided that their money had all but run out. Unless she could find a considerable sum within the next day, the family would probably lose their home and we would all be homeless.

Without hesitation, I made my way to my maid's room and counted the bundles of cash I held squirrelled in the recesses of my bed. I had the exact amount Marta needed. Triumphant, I emerged from my room carrying the bundles of cash like a paper-shaped hug. She refused my offer at first, but I said it was the least I could do in return for the kindness she had shown me in my hour of need. Eventually she accepted, on condition that the sum be treated as a loan and repaid as soon as good fortune returned.

Then one day, we heard of the murder of María Moyano, a community organizer in the Villa El Salvador ward in the slums, who was shot at close range then blown up with dynamite.

She, like many Peruvian women, was trying to keep serving local communities' needs, organising food kitchens and glasses of milk for the poor, but for the Shining Path this was counter-revolutionary and not the way to bring about change. Maria Moyano led a group of activists called Women's Federation. She was deemed a great threat to the

Maoist revolutionaries as she frequently spoke out against us, labelling us terrorists.

This woman was admirable in her strength and in her love for her people. Her violent death led to public outcry and her funeral was attended by thousands of people from all over the country. I understood that communities would feel outraged, as she was a friend of the poor. But I knew Guzmán could not allow the cancer of dissent to grow in the cities, and that is why he had sent in Jorge and his men to stamp it out by eliminating one of their leaders.

Shortly after this incident, Lima exploded into a frenzy once again. Guzmán was arrested in broad daylight in a safehouse in Comas, minutes from where the Ramirez family lived, in a residence operating as a ballet studio. The military police routinely searched the garbage taken out from the house and had found discarded tubes of cream for the treatment of psoriasis, an ailment that Guzmán was known to have. An elite unit raided the residence, where they found and arrested Guzmán and eight others, including my rival, Elena Iparraguirre.

In the countryside there was a legend that when he felt surrounded, Guzmán would turn into a bird, a snake, or a stone, so that he would be left alone and escape. In some villages, schoolchildren were said to draw pictures of colourful red birds called Comrade Gonzalo, whom they said could fly over entire mountain ranges without ever getting caught. There were versions of Guzmán to suit all tastes. But this time, it seemed he had been found and captured in his human form.

Men and women disappear but ideas live on, and with Guzmán gone his followers would be thinking through what to do next. With only five thousand combatants, one of the greatest revolutionary fires in history had shone bright and fierce for almost fifteen years, then it had lost its leader and was burning out.

But from my side, I simply found myself reflecting on the meaning of kindness. The ideology I had built my life upon had turned into a great meat grinder, churning thousands of lives in its wake. The bourgeois oppressor I had existed to fight had become my closest family and we had supported each other through hardship like equals. For now, it was time to put down my weapons and lower my guard. I had found my home.

Part 4 – Rosa's story

Ayahuasca

(Teacher Plant)

For three years I stayed in Santa Monica prison, sleeping, yearning, crying and listening to the memories of the dead. My days were punctuated by routine and illuminated by weekly visits from Emanuel and the children. The twins were growing up fast, and they seemed confident and strong. They would arrive at visiting times, immaculately turned out – teeth shining, hair plaited and smoothed, clothes crisp and ironed, and shoes shined and dust-free. They would bring delicious home-cooked food to show me how well the family were being looked after in my absence. If they bore a grudge against me for abandoning them, or shame for what others thought of me, they never let this show. I was not worried about the twins – they had interconnected minds and were never lonely.

The twins were born white as snow due to the shock I had suffered from the bomb explosion during my pregnancy. But in every other respect, they could not have been more different. Rosita was short and plump and bubbled with eternal optimism like her father, whilst Roxana was taller and willowy, and had a melancholy streak. But they were inseparable and looked out for each other at every turn. They were never envious or jealous. As they entered their teenage years, if a boy were courting one the other would insist on spending a day with him to ensure he was suitable for her sister. They knew each other's thoughts and finished each other's sentences. In my absence, they even stopped each other from eating avocado to protect their virtue. No, the twins were strong, and they gave me nothing to worry about. It was my gay son I lost sleep over. At night I would toss and turn thinking of what misfortunes he might be facing.

When I was free, I had spent my days defending him tooth and nail against slander and mockery from young men in the slums. Being gay was no laughing matter in those days. Either you kept it secret and pretended to be interested in girls, or you took the path of self-destruction as a transvestite like Ricardo, who had gone to school with my children but now frequented the seedy bars and brothels in the centre of Lima. Ricardo would appear at dawn in the slum, returning to his mother's house when most of us were setting off for our jobs as domestic servants or security guards. He dressed extravagantly with high heels and tight clothes, pitifully thin and haggard and obviously on drugs. The men would whistle and hurl insults at him, and he would mince by, smiling wearily at them. My son Jaime too was effeminate, but I encouraged him to stand up for himself, to stay away from Ricardo and to dream big. We chatted often, laughing and plotting as accomplices do. Our big ambition was that he would escape the slums to become an air steward and live in style in New York.

Now I was powerless to defend him from the confines of my cell, and I lay fretting about him, praying and asking incessantly after him. My nights were long and punctuated by worry for Jaime. When I did sleep, my dreams began to close in on me. I accessed the memories of so many dead when I drifted to sleep in my prison cell. This power had been granted to me when I was very young, but I must have been too busy to take notice, or perhaps my mind had not been open to it. But now, in the empty hours at night, with nothing but the faint noises of snoring and creaking beds from other prisoners, and the buzz of crickets beyond the prison walls, I had all the time in the world to listen.

Some memories belonged to people I had known in my youth and adulthood, but many were complete strangers who just left images and glimpses of their lives with me as they floated by. It was as though they were dropping a handkerchief in their paths, and I would follow them to pick it up. One woman was pouring memories into my nightly dreams. I could not be sure who she was at first, and I could not see her face. But I was visited by images of her childhood in the Amazon, which felt familiar. Her childhood seemed like mine – a snippet of conversation, the grainy memory of a family meal, the rustling of leaves as a small child made her way through the woods.

When she was older, the memories grew more bittersweet. There were acrid smells and fear and furtiveness. She had found the love of her life, but he was caught up in cocaine production. I saw her husband dig a deep hole in the ground and hide sack after sack of what I knew was base cocaine. This woman escaped to Lima for a new life, where I could sense her finding new meaning. She had become an activist fighting for the rights of the poor and the oppressed. She sought to meet their needs and satisfy their hunger. Her memories had now become loud and outspoken and they raged with indignation. Then one night the worst happened. The terrorists had her killed. Gunshot rang out and echoed through my sleep, and an explosion shattered any last memories. I woke suddenly as the blast echoed through my broken slumber, gasping and covered in sweat. With horror, I realised that these images all belonged to my dear friend from the Glass of Milk committee, Maria Moyano.

Trembling with shock, I emerged from my cell and tried to find out what had happened to Maria. The wardens were supposed to keep newspapers away from us due to the risk of enticing terrorist activities, but I had earned their respect. I was given clippings covering the killing from a few months earlier. I was horrified by the way Maria had been shot and blown up, a violent, barbaric death for such a beautiful soul. I cried for many days in my cell, refusing to eat or drink as I processed the news. I could barely imagine what the tragedy would have done to our community. But I drew comfort from reading that thousands of people had attended her funeral and processed through the streets of Lima in her honour, showing love and support for her work and for what she represented. Her memory would live on, and I knew that her spirit would continue to fight despite what the terrorist cowards had done to her.

After crying for six days I finally fell into a deep, refreshing sleep. I saw Maria in peace, smiling as she contemplated the gates of heaven. "The garden of Eden is like our jungle, dear Rosa, but with even sweeter fruit!" She laughed as she bade me goodbye. "Don't lose heart. Soon you will be free again and we will win this fight, just wait and see."

I woke up the next morning and decided to move on with my life. Washing my face, I made my way out of the cell for morning chores. My fellow inmates were busy making jewellery, knitting hats or preparing cakes and elaborate dishes, ready to sell on visiting days. I walked around the courtyard and stopped to greet my friends working in the hairdressing salon, the library and the school. There was Francesca, a large Dutch lady who had been stopped at the airport. She was given 30 years when her suitcase was found to contain fifty kilos of white powder. She scrubbed the prison toilets assiduously four times a day and her sentence had been reduced by half due to good behaviour.

"I was on drugs back in Holland, and homeless and desperate," she told me. "One easy trip to Peru, and they said I could make enough to pay my debts and get my children out of care."

But now, a monthly letter with some pictures was her only contact with the children. Francesca and I had become good friends, and she would join me when my twins came to visit, hugging them tearfully as they were the same age as her own.

"Never take drugs!" she would order them in her broken Spanish. And to me she said, "You must be strong. You are innocent and your beautiful family is waiting for you."

There were so many women like Francesca in the prison, and we worked and cooked and cried and dreamed together as the days slowly crept by.

A year after I had said my goodbyes to Maria, another woman began occupying my dreams. Her memories were tumultuous and dark and driven by hatred. Unlike all the other people I had dreamt of, this woman was still alive, and I could see snippets of her daily life as well as waves of memories from her past.

She lived in Lima and was caring for someone else's house and children, but she had grown up in the mountains of the South. In my dreams I felt her childhood influences, and the biting cold and eternal ice of the Andes. I noticed the poverty and hunger of those around her, and the surge of anger and strife as her family put their hope into communism. She had become a very powerful figure amongst the insurgent forces tearing through our country like a raging wind. She hated those in power yet was also full of love for the oppressed and the poor. I did not know who she was, but she returned to me night after night.

As my time in prison dragged on, I eavesdropped in my dreams that this woman was behind Maria's killing. She and her partner in crime, a man of great power, had ordered Maria's slaughter to keep her quiet. I also found, as her memories continued to dominate my nights, that she was responsible for the death of my family, all those years ago in the jungle. I was faint with dread, but I knew this was all true. These dreams were unlike any I had had before. They carried the detail of a recent conversation, like the vividness of a moon on a clear night.

When I awoke, the air in my cell felt heavy, like being at the bottom of a lake. I got up, shivering with fear but quite sure of what I needed to do. If I could see people's pasts in my dreams, perhaps I could also reach out to them. I would tell this woman that I knew what she had done.

I thought about the injustice of our situation. I was innocent but languishing in prison for a crime I had not committed. Maria, who had fought for the oppressed and brought happiness to many, had been blown up mercilessly by her enemies. And the woman who was guilty of having Maria and so many others killed, was still free and in hiding in Lima, almost close enough to touch.

For this next dream I would need some extra help, and I approached one of my inmates, Ines, who was known for her shamanic past. I asked her for a small dose of ayahuasca vine, the "teacher plant" used by my people as the gateway to the spiritual world and its secrets. Although Ines was in prison for illicit activities, selling ayahuasca was not one of them – the government claimed that consumption of the teacher plant constituted one of the basic pillars of the identity of the Amazon peoples and that it should be legalised, and respected. So she prepared a concoction for me, mixing the plant with a paste made from bitter chacruna plant and boiling it with cinnamon to mask its foul aroma, then blessing it before I took a sip.

I spent several hours in a conscious but dream-like state, waiting for the woman in hiding to fall asleep so that I could find her and speak to her. Eventually, as my breathing became calm and regular, I began to feel her breathing too. I knew that she could hear me, even though I still didn't know who she was.

"I know what you have done to so many innocent people."
I spoke clearly, without fear or anger, aware of the thread
of humanity that bound us together. "You have killed and
ordered men to kill relentlessly in the name of your ideals.
Because of you, my own family died – and my best friend too.
Unless you repent, I will make sure these people live in your
dreams for the rest of your days."

I would love to be able to say that I saw the woman or heard
her weep with regret and repent on the spot – but I did
not. I was under the powerful effect of the ayahuasca and
at that point began to hallucinate madly before vomiting
uncontrollably into a small bucket. This, Ines reassured me,
was the teacher plant opening my mind and healing all my
past trauma.

During the remainder of my time in prison I did not dream
of the woman again, but I felt serene in the knowledge that
she had understood my message and would somehow make
amends.

A lawyer came to visit me soon after this incident. Emanuel
had previously contracted one, but we could only afford to
go to the dubious firms on the side of the dusty Pachacutec
road, where they sold you the promise of resolving all your
concerns in exchange for thirty dollars. A nervous looking
young man visited me with a notebook and shrugged his
shoulders when he heard my story. "I don't think we can get
you out, senora," he mumbled nervously before disappearing

back to his office. Soon afterwards Emanuel was told the thirty-dollar fee covered one prison visit and that nothing further could be done – not until we could produce "further evidence" of my innocence and pay the law firm many more dollars.

But this lawyer was different. She was dressed smartly and had the haughty confidence of someone from San Isidro, the most privileged part of the city. She arrived wearing a sharp pencil skirt and crisp white shirt, her hair swept back into a neat bun. She shook my hand warmly and told me that someone had sent her to help me. I had no idea who would do such a thing – Senora Sanchez was the only rich person I had known and would surely have been indifferent to my fate. But I was lonely and desperate, and this mysterious new lawyer represented my only hope.

Her name was Irina and she said she could make no promises, but that with patience and hard work we could probably prove that I had been unaware of the cocaine placed in my shipment, and get my prison sentence down to a couple of years. I hugged Irina tight, smothering her elegant young face with my tears and crumpling her crisp shirt as I thanked her – and praised God for sending her to me. It no longer mattered if He was the God of the Catholics or of the American missionaries in smart suits – my prayers were being answered and one day I would be free again.

Emanuel and the children came to visit me the next morning

for breakfast. We celebrated the news with copious amounts of Juanes – ground corn wrapped in banana leaves – which the twins had pounded, folded and boiled the night before knowing they were my favourite jungle delicacy. I told them all about Irina and we all cried with relief into our fragrant Juanes.

"But who sent her and who is going to pay her?" Emanuel kept asking in disbelief. The only option we could think of was that the Mexicans, filled with remorse, had used some of the cocaine money to contract Irina's services. It seemed very unlikely, and this prospect also brought its own set of worries. If they were bailing me out would they then claim control over us and demand we take part in further cocaine deals? Would they be standing at the door when I left prison, claiming ownership over me and over my family forever afterwards? I tried to get Irina to reveal who my mysterious benefactor was, but she said she did not know. So, deciding I had nothing to lose, I let her get on with the job.

For two years Irina worked tirelessly on my behalf. Eventually she put together a strong case, arguing that I would never knowingly have jeopardised my family and that my lack of prior conviction and my strong work ethic warranted a faster release. The Judge at Lima's central court looked wearily at me. He saw hundreds of these cases every week. He listened intently while Irina outlined every detail of my unfortunate situation. With a perfunctory wave of the hand, he acquitted me, urging me to be more responsible and to keep a better eye on any future shipments to Mexico.

On the day of my release, I said goodbye to my inmates as I waited for my family to pick me up. I felt elated and nervous, like a celebrity waiting for the rolling out of the red carpet and the silver flash of the cameras. I had grown fond of the women in the prison – Ines and her magic, big Francesca and her tragic drug stories from Holland, and all the others from the hairdressing salon, the library and the school. I hugged the women tearfully as we promised to be reunited soon on the other side.

I knew I was one of the lucky ones. I was returning to my family, to my home in the dusty sand banks of the slums, ready to rebuild our lives and our country. We were not the army, the terrorists or the drug traffickers, but we were the great victors of the bloody war our nation had gone through – because we were alive, and we were free. I had forgiven my family's killers and I had Maria's strength to carry me forward.

When Guzmán, the leader of the Shining Path was finally arrested and put behind two-metre-thick walls a few months later, everyone looked for his wife and right-hand woman Comrade Norah, also known as Augusta La Torre. A massive manhunt ensued. Pictures of Augusta La Torre were plastered all over Lima and a family came forward, the Ramirez. They said she had been their maid for years, and that they had had no idea who she was.

She had given them no reason for suspicion and had worked for them faithfully, they said – saving her wages and at one point bailing them out of near-bankruptcy. Gratefully they had paid her back, and the newspapers said she had then used the money to secure a good lawyer and get a good friend out of prison.

Augusta was never seen again, but I knew that I was the friend she had referred to, and that Augusta La Torre was the one who had paid Irina to get me out of prison. I carried on talking to Augusta in my dreams for many years, never knowing if she could really hear me or not, where she was, or indeed whether she was dead or alive.

Sometimes I dreamt of her as a small girl, laughing at a bull run whilst nestling in her father's arms. Sometimes I saw her running through the jungle, armed and fearless like an Amazon warrior. And sometimes she seemed to be calling me from a cold land in the distant North, full of snow and ice, and pine trees and red houses. But I could never really be sure. When I woke up, I would tell Emanuel, Jaime and the twins, but they all just laughed at me.

Epilogue

Canada: Immigration and Refugee Board of Canada, *Peru: Information on Augusta La Torre, wife of Abimael Guzmán*, 1 January 1993, PER12684, available at: https://www.refworld.org/docid/3ae6ad9710.html [accessed 23 May 2020]

According to the available sources, Augusta la Torre was known within the Shining Path organization as comrade Norah and is presumed dead. She is thought to have played a crucial role in the leadership of the Shining Path since its inception, with some arguing that she may have encouraged Abimael Guzmán to put his theories into practice. Augusta La Torre reportedly encouraged her husband to found the Popular Women's Movement in 1965 in the city of Ayacucho. This movement reportedly "produced the theoretical context for the role of women in the movement" publishing booklets and a magazine in Quechua and Spanish.

Augusta La Torre reportedly headed the female branch of the Maoist group Bandera Roja (Red Flag) and was one of the founders of Socorro Popular (Popular Succour), a front organization. In 1989 Augusta La Torre and Abimael Guzmán may have been separated, with her possibly being the person responsible for foreign activities of the Shining Path. Relatives of Augusta La Torre who are also reported to be involved in the Shining Path have apparently been residing and carrying out political activity in Sweden. Javier Esparza Marquez, married to Augusta's sister Gisela, is a long-time militant of the Shining Path who is or has been the group's representative in that country.

One source states that Augusta La Torre died on 14 November 1989. Based on documents found by the Peruvian police in a Shining Path safehouse that was raided in January 1991, another source states that Augusta La Torre may have been dead by 29 June 1989. According to this source, a "congress" of the Shining Path leadership agreed to award comrade Nora on 29 June 1989 the "order of the hammer and sickle" which, according to the source, is the highest tribute awarded by the Shining Path.

The same magazine reported earlier that the videotaped wake of a dead woman, whom Abimael Guzmán is seen kissing and giving a speech for, was that of Augusta La Torre. The wake may have taken place in early 1990, and the body may have been buried in the garden of a house in the Lima district of Comas. Based on information contained in the same videotape, another source reports that Augusta La Torre died at the age of 43, after 26 year of militancy in the Shining Path.

The same source speculates on the possible death or suicide of Augusta La Torre, although no clear conclusion is reached in the article.

Printed in Great Britain
by Amazon

21685610R00072